Wild Highway

USA TODAY BESTSELLING AUTHOR
DEVNEY PERRY

WILD HIGHWAY

Copyright © 2020 by Devney Perry LLC

ISBN: 978-1-950692-22-4

Editing & Proofreading:

Marion Archer, Making Manuscripts

www.makingmanuscripts.com

Julie Deaton, Deaton Author Services

www.facebook.com/jdproofs

Karen Lawson, The Proof is in the Reading

Judy Zweifel, Judy's Proofreading

www.judysproofreading.com

Cover:

Sarah Hansen © Okay Creations

www.okaycreations.com

ALSO BY DEVNEY PERRY

Jamison Valley Series

The Coppersmith Farmhouse

The Clover Chapel

The Lucky Heart

The Outpost

The Bitterroot Inn

The Candle Palace

Maysen Jar Series

The Birthday List

Letters to Molly

Lark Cove Series

Tattered

Timid

Tragic

Tinsel

Tin Gypsy Series

Gypsy King

Riven Knight

Stone Princess

Noble Prince

Runaway Series

Runaway Road

Wild Highway

Quarter Miles

Standalones

Rifts and Refrains

CHAPTER ONE

GEMMA

"I'm sorry, what did you say? Where are you? Kansas? As in Dorothy and Toto? That Kansas?" Benjamin's string of questions came in his signature style—rapid-fire. "What happened to West Virginia?"

"I was in West Virginia," I said into the phone. "Now I'm in Kansas."

"B-but *why?*"

I didn't need to see his face to know it was agape with shock. For too long, Benjamin had tracked my every move. He'd stood by my side as I'd created my empire and had executed my directives with precision. The rigidity of my schedule wasn't just for my benefit. He'd managed it flawlessly for the past six years.

This trip of mine was going to freak him way the hell out.

"I have something important to tell you."

"No." He groaned. "I'm still dealing with the mess you left me the last time you had something important to tell me."

"Sorry." I hadn't meant to shake up his world. But since I'd completely torpedoed mine, changes to his were inevitable.

Three weeks ago, I'd called Benjamin into my office and told him that I was no longer the CEO of Gemma Lane. That I'd sold my beloved cosmetics company and namesake to Procter & Gamble. The monster corporation had purchased my brand and skin care formulas for the bargain price of twelve million dollars.

The sale had been a spur-of-the-moment decision. I didn't make those, not anymore. And ever since, I'd been waiting for a ping of regret. It hadn't hit me yet.

Instead, I'd felt free.

Selling Gemma Lane had been the first spontaneous decision I'd made in years. The floodgates were open now and these past three weeks had seen countless decisions made entirely with personal motivations.

For eleven years, I'd given every shred of my concentration and energy to my businesses. I'd worked my ass off to make sure I'd never be poor or homeless or hungry again. I'd lived my life with extreme control, shutting out any added emotion that wouldn't increase my bottom line.

Then I'd just . . . walked away.

All because of a pasta and breadsticks lunch with a former colleague.

I'd gotten a random phone call from my friend Julie. She'd worked with me selling real estate years before and we'd loosely kept in touch over the years. Neither of us had stayed in real estate, and while I'd chosen to create my own company, she'd worked her way up the executive ranks at Procter & Gamble.

We'd met for lunch to celebrate her recent promotion. And she'd asked me, point-blank, if I'd ever sell Gemma Lane. The word *yes* came from nowhere, shocking us both. We'd negotiated over the meal and Julie had taken my bottom-line number to her superiors.

Five hours later, I had the legal agreement in my inbox.

My life had flown out the window, like a ream of paper being tossed from my fourteenth-floor office on a windy day. Benjamin had been trying to catch the pages and stack them neatly again, except I just kept tossing more.

"I'm taking some time away," I told him.

"In West Virginia. You're supposed to be in West Virginia visiting Londyn. Wait, what's that noise? Are you driving?"

"Yes. About that . . ." My best friend Londyn was the reason I was in this car. "I was in West Virginia visiting Londyn. But remember last year when I told you she was taking her Cadillac and driving it to California?"

"I do. Except she met Brooks in West Virginia and married him. What does this—" Benjamin stopped. He was a brilliant man and normally our conversations went this way—I'd start explaining and he'd jump to the end before I could finish my story. "No. Tell me you're not taking this car to California yourself."

"I'm taking the car to California myself."

"Are you serious? You're driving from West Virginia to California? Alone?"

"Yes, yes and yes." I held my breath as the line went silent.

"You really have lost your goddamn mind."

I laughed. "You're not wrong."

"Gemma, what is going on with you?" The concern in his voice tugged at my heart. "Is this a you-turned-thirty-this-year crisis? Should I call Dr. Brewer?"

"No." I didn't need my therapist getting involved. Dr. Brewer would dredge up the past, and my childhood was the last thing I wanted to discuss at the moment. "It was just time for a change."

"A change? This is not a change. This is a nuclear explosion. You sold the company. Your baby. Gemma Lane was your *life*. You were there five in the morning until eight at night every single day. Now it's gone."

I nodded, waiting for him to continue. This wasn't the first time he'd reminded me of exactly what I'd done. Yet, I still didn't feel like I'd made a huge mistake.

"Two weeks ago, you handed me an entirely new list of job duties, including managing all your assets and capital ventures while you disappeared to West Virginia. Now you're driving to California? This isn't you."

"But it used to be," I said.

I used to be impulsive and adventurous. Money and success were to blame for the caution that had invaded my life. A month ago, I'd had hundreds of employees counting on me to make the right decisions. They'd needed me to take care with my actions to ensure they had jobs. In worrying about them—for hours, days, years—I'd lost myself.

Now those employees would be working for Procter & Gamble. It had been part of my agreement that every one of my employees had future employment. Except for Benjamin. He'd always worked for me personally.

"I need this," I confessed. "I used to be fun. I used to be daring and reckless. You wouldn't even recognize that version of me."

Benjamin had only known the Gemma consumed by work. He didn't recognize me without the meetings, conference calls and galas. He didn't see that the charity balls I used to love—the ones where I'd smile as I sipped champagne because Boston's elite had let a lowly, runaway kid into their midst—were now suffocating and dull.

"Where is this coming from?" Benjamin asked. "I'm not buying this 'I needed a change' explanation. Something happened and you haven't told me."

Yes, something had happened, and I hadn't told anyone, not even Londyn. "Remember Jason Jensen?"

"The guy who used to work in marketing?"

"Yes. He asked me to marry him."

"What?" he shouted, the volume making me wince. "When? How long were you dating? How did I not know about this?"

"We dated for a few months. Obviously, we didn't tell anyone because I was his boss's boss. We agreed to keep it quiet, and I didn't think we were serious. But then one night about a month ago, he took me to this fancy restaurant, got down on one knee and proposed."

"Oh, Gemma. I'm sorry." As always, Benjamin jumped to the end of my story.

"Don't pity me. Pity Jason. He was sweet and handsome and kind. But I just . . . I couldn't say yes. I didn't love him."

So in a restaurant full of people watching, I'd broken a good man's heart.

"That's why he quit," Benjamin said.

"Yeah."

The day Jason had left, I'd sat in my office alone, giving him space to pack his things and say goodbye to his coworkers. I'd stared out my wall of windows and wished I'd loved him.

He was gracious and caring. Jason hadn't hated me for turning him down, he just couldn't work for me any longer. I didn't fault him for that. He'd loved unselfishly, not complaining that I'd been in the spotlight.

And I'd felt nothing but guilt.

"He just wasn't the right guy," Benjamin said. "That doesn't mean you had to sell your company, your car and your brownstone. You gave up your life."

"Was it really that good of a life?"

He sighed. "So what now?"

"I'm taking a road trip in this incredible car. Then . . . I don't know." Most of my belongings had either been donated to charity or put into storage. My house I'd sold furnished. What I had fit into the trunk of this car, and for today, it was enough.

I'd deal with tomorrow, well . . . tomorrow.

"What can I do?"

I smiled. Maybe Benjamin didn't understand what I was doing, but he'd support me, nonetheless. "Exactly what you are doing."

He was managing my assets, paying my bills and dealing with any questions that came up with my other business ventures. It was all work I'd done myself before the sale. It had been the second job I hadn't needed but something to fill the lonely nights. Work had always been my forte.

Now I'd handed it over to Benjamin.

Since he no longer had to manage my hectic calendar and activities at Gemma Lane, he'd watch over my numerous real estate holdings, acting as the liaison to the property management company I'd hired years ago. Benjamin would step in and be the go-between with my financial managers.

The restaurants that had needed my influx of cash to get up and running were now some of Boston's finest. They ran on autopilot. I owned an interest in a car dealership, one that peddled foreign luxury as opposed to the classic Americana I was currently driving. And I was also a partner in a fashion design company, the one that had designed the black sweater I was currently wearing along with a handful of others packed in my suitcase.

Benjamin would ensure we received regular profit and loss reports from my investments along with my annual dividends, then alert me to any red flags.

"Okay," he said. "It will be in good hands until you get back."

I bit my tongue, because as the open road stretched before me, there was a good chance I wouldn't be back. I was on a new path now. Where it was going, I wasn't sure. But the excitement, the freedom, was something I hadn't felt in a long, long time.

"Call if you need anything. And, Benjamin?"

"Yeah?"

"Thank you."

"Drive safely."

I tossed my phone aside and put both hands on the white steering wheel.

Londyn's cherry-red, 1964 Cadillac DeVille convertible was a dream to drive. The car sailed down the interstate, the wheels skimming over the asphalt as the body sliced through the air.

She'd paid a small fortune to restore this car from the rusted heap it had once been. Gone were the torn, flat seats. They'd been replaced with thick cushions covered with buttery, white leather that matched the wheel. The air-conditioning kept the cab from getting too hot, and when I felt like blasting music, the sound system was deafening.

This car's look was different but the inside would always feel like Londyn's home. As an old, abandoned wreck destined for the scrap pile, Londyn had chosen this Cadillac as her shelter in a junkyard we'd called home.

The junkyard in Temecula, California, where Londyn, four other kids and I had lived after running away from our respective homes.

The six of us had made our own family in that junkyard. I hadn't lived in a car, instead choosing to build myself a makeshift tent. I'd tried to talk Londyn into a tent or structure too so she'd have more space, but she'd fallen in love with the car.

And with Karson.

He'd lived in this car with her while they'd been together. Londyn hadn't seen him since we'd moved away from California, but he was the reason she'd set out to take this car to California in the first place.

Karson would always hold a special place in her heart. He'd been her first love. He'd been our friend. He'd always hold a special place in mine too. Londyn had wanted him to have this car and see it restored to its former glory. That, and I think she wanted to know that he was all right.

If delivering the Cadillac to him would make her happy, I'd gladly drive the miles.

And I could use the time to figure out my next move.

Figure out who I wanted to be.

I glanced at myself in the rearview mirror. My chocolate-brown hair was piled in a messy knot on top of my head. I hadn't bothered with makeup in my hotel room this morning. I looked a far cry from the corporate tycoon I'd been last month.

Gone were the posh and polish. They were somewhere in the miles behind me, strewn across the interstate.

I'd left West Virginia two days ago, heeding Londyn's advice not to rush the trip. The first day, I'd driven for six hours before stopping in Louisville, Kentucky, for the night. I'd eaten dinner alone, not unusual for me, then went to bed. The next day, I'd crossed into Missouri for a stop in Kansas City. Then this morning, I'd awoken refreshed and ready to hit the road.

So here I was, hours later, in the middle of Kansas on a warm September day.

Flat fields spread like a golden ocean in every direction, only disturbed by the occasional barn or building.

The road stretched in an endless line in front of me and rarely did I have to turn the steering wheel. Traffic on the interstate was crowded with semitrucks hauling loads across the country.

As the day wore on, I found myself relaxing to the whir of the tires on the pavement. I studied the landscape and its subtle changes as I approached the border to Colorado. And I breathed.

Truly breathed.

There were no emails to return. No calls to answer. No decisions to make. Benjamin would deal with any emergency that came up. As of now, I was the blissfully silent partner.

Walking away from my life had been relatively easy.

What did that mean? What did it mean that the only person who'd called me since leaving Boston was my paid employee?

Lost in my head, it took me a moment to notice the flash of red and blue lights racing up behind me. When their flicker caught my eye, my heart jumped to my throat and my foot instantly came off the gas. My hands gripped the wheel at ten and two as I glanced at the speedometer.

"Shit. Don't pull me over. Please, please, please." The last thing I needed was another speeding ticket.

The police car zoomed into the passing lane and streaked by. The air rushed from my lungs and I watched him disappear down the road ahead.

Thank God. I set the cruise control to exactly the speed limit.

Why did I always speed? When the limit was seventy-five, why did I push it to eighty-nine? When was I going to learn to slow down?

I'd never excelled at going slow or taking my time. I'd always put in twenty times the effort as others because I hadn't had an Ivy League education or family pedigree to rely on. But give me a dollar and I'd turn it into ten through sheer will and determination. I worked hard and fast, something I'd been doing since running away from home at sixteen.

If you wanted to survive on the streets, you didn't act slow. I'd figured out quickly how to care for myself. Granted, I'd had help. In the beginning, Karson had been my lifeline.

He and I had lived in the same shitty neighborhood. As kids, he'd walked with me to school and had played with me at the neighborhood park. It was a miracle neither of us had contracted tetanus from the swing set. Whenever I ran from my home crying, I'd often find him at that park, avoiding his own home.

Karson had been my closest friend. The day he hadn't showed up at school, I'd gone to check on him. When I'd peeked through his window and saw his backpack was missing, I'd known he'd finally had enough.

When I'd hit the same breaking point, I'd sought him out. There hadn't been a lot of other options. Karson had already made the junkyard his home. Then he'd helped make it mine.

A month later, Londyn came along. I'd found her digging through a Dumpster behind a restaurant, picking off a piece of wilted lettuce from a sandwich and actually opening her mouth to eat the damn thing. I gagged remembering that stench.

I'd ripped that sandwich out of her hand and tossed it back in the trash where it had belonged.

We'd been best friends ever since.

After saving her from the sandwich, I'd hauled her to the junkyard, made her a peanut butter and jelly, and introduced her to Karson. It had taken them three months to finally admit they liked each other. And another three months before Karson began spending his nights in her Cadillac.

A lot had changed since then. Life had split us all apart, though Londyn and I had always stayed friends. We'd both spent years living in Boston, meeting for drinks and manicures on a weekly basis. But Boston hadn't been right, for either of us.

I was happy she'd found Brooks and a home in West Virginia. Had the others found happiness too? A few years ago—driven by curiosity or nostalgia or both—I'd hired a private investigator to look everyone up. It had taken him a few months since I hadn't given him much to start with besides names, but he'd found them. Karson had still been in California, Clara in Arizona, and Aria in Oregon.

And Katherine was in Montana, where I'd left her behind.

The sound of my ringing phone startled me and I stretched to grab it from the passenger seat, seeing Londyn's name on the screen.

"I was just thinking about you," I answered.

"Good things?"

"I was thinking about how we met."

"You mean how you saved me from food poisoning and ultimate starvation?"

I laughed. "Yep."

"Ah, good times." She giggled. "How's the trip?"

In the background, I heard her husband, Brooks. "Ask her if the car is running okay."

"Did you hear him?" she asked.

"Yeah. Tell him it's running fine."

"She says there's a strange knocking sound every few minutes. And if she gives it too much gas at once, the whole car lurches."

"What?" His voice echoed to my ear. "I just tuned it up. Give me that phone."

I laughed at the sound of her swatting him away.

"I'm kidding," she told him. "The car is fine. Now go away so we can talk. Ellie needs her diaper changed. I saved it just for you."

"Gee, thanks," he muttered. Through the phone, I recognized the sound of a soft kiss.

Jealousy would be easy if I wasn't so happy for her.

"Where are you?" she asked.

"I crossed into Colorado about twenty miles ago. I'm hoping to get to Denver tonight. Then maybe tomorrow, I'll put in a long stretch and see if I can get to Las Vegas."

Londyn sighed. "There's no hurry, Gem. Why don't you stay in Colorado for a week? Explore and relax."

"Maybe." Did I even know how to relax?

"When was the last time you took a weekend off?"

"Um . . ." It hadn't been in recent years. "Montana, I guess."

"That was—what?—eleven years ago? I'd say you're overdue," she said. "So you were thinking about the junk-yard days, huh? Why?"

"I don't know. Reminiscing, I guess. Wondering where do I go after this trip. Things were hard, but life seemed easier back at Lou's."

Lou Miley had owned the junkyard where the six of us kids had lived. He'd been a loner and a gruff old man. Unfriendly and irritable. But he'd let us stay without question.

"Are you okay?" Londyn asked. "Should I be worried?"

"No," I promised. "I was just thinking about how we all scattered. Everyone but Karson. I wonder how everyone is doing."

"You're still upset about the Katherine thing, aren't you?"

"I screwed up."

Londyn sighed. "You were nineteen years old and jumped at an opportunity to make some money. I highly doubt she holds it against you. Considering where we all came from, Katherine, above all people, couldn't fault you for wanting to better your life."

"I don't know," I mumbled.

I'd broken a promise to a close friend. I'd ditched her, choosing money over that promise and the decision had haunted me since.

This was a fresh start for me. There was nothing holding me back. Londyn wanted me to take an overdue vacation. Maybe what I really needed before I could concentrate on the future, was to make an overdue apology for a past mistake.

An idea stirred in my mind, calling and demanding some attention. It was like a flashing light, one that would keep blinking until I gave it my focus. This feeling was familiar, and usually, it meant another successful business venture.

But not this time.

This idea had nothing to do with money.

"Would you care if it took me longer than planned to get the Cadillac to Karson?" Because my intuition was screaming at me to take a massive detour.

"Nope," she said. "It's your trip. Make the most of it."

"Okay." I smiled. "Thanks, Lonny."

"Of course. Call me soon."

"Bye." The moment I ended the call, I pulled up my digital map and punched in a new destination.

These spontaneous decisions of the past few weeks suddenly made sense. They had purpose. They had meaning. They were to get me here, in this moment.

I was setting out to right a wrong. To find myself again.

On the wild highway.

CHAPTER TWO

GEMMA

I'd forgotten the majesty of Montana. I'd forgotten how vast the state was. How the landscapes changed from savage prairie to rugged forest as you traveled from one side to the other.

The last time I'd traveled through Montana, it had been on a bus destined for Boston. Back then, I'd cursed the driver for taking the trip at such a lazy pace. This time, I'd let myself find excuses to slow down.

In the past five days, I'd made a conscious effort to drive unhurried. Mostly, it was to avoid a ticket. But there was also a part of me nervous about seeing Katherine again, and that anxiety had given me plenty of excuses to stop along the way.

My journey had taken me north, through Colorado and Wyoming. I'd spent last night in Missoula, not wanting to arrive at the ranch at dinnertime. Really, I was a coward and had needed one more night to work up the courage for what I was about to do.

So I'd stayed in town and found a cheap nail salon for a last-minute mani-pedi. This morning, I'd taken care with my appearance, going for the makeup treatment and adding loose waves to my long hair.

The tattered boyfriend jeans I'd been wearing on repeat were traded for a pair of dark wash skinnies. My green sweater brought out the caramel flecks in my hazel eyes and my tan booties had enough of a heel that they took my outfit from casual to chic.

Still, I'd wished for one of my designer suits.

I'd worn blazers, pencil skirts and six-inch heels, almost exclusively, over the past decade. Since leaving West Virginia, my laid-back attire of jeans, oversized sweaters and sandals had been an adjustment. I didn't feel prepared. Powerful.

My wardrobe in Boston had become an armor of sorts. When I'd walked into the office in a suit, my hair twisted into a tight chignon, no one had questioned who was in charge. I needed that armor today—a bit of the old Gemma to help me get through this.

But the suits were all in storage. Today, I had to face this without airs. I'd be vulnerable. Humble. Sincere. Because today wasn't about conquering the world or turning a profit. Today was about making things right with a friend.

The trees along the road were changing. Stark yellow

and orange leaves popped against an evergreen backdrop. The fall air was crisp and, if I hadn't spent time on my hair this morning, I would have driven with the convertible's top down.

The miles disappeared too quickly and when the first sign for the Greer Ranch and Mountain Resort came into view, my stomach somersaulted.

I could do this. I had to do this. I hadn't made many apologies, lately. Arrogant as it was, I did my best not to screw up, and for the most part, I had a good track record.

This would bruise my ego but would be worth it.

I turned off the highway, my heart pounding, and traversed the gravel road that led from the highway toward the lodge. Being here, on this road, took me back to another lifetime. I struggled to keep my eyes on the road as I took it all in. The mountains. The meadows. The buildings coming into view past a grove of trees.

It was exactly as I'd remembered. In the past decade, the Greer Ranch hadn't seemed to change.

The lodge was a rustic log building and the focal point for guests—or it had been when I'd worked here. Behind it was an enormous barn beside a doubly enormous stable.

All three were the same, rich brown color. The windows of the lodge gleamed in the morning Montana sunshine. Maroon and golden mums spilled from a toppled whiskey barrel beside the front steps. Three wooden rocking chairs were positioned to the left of the hand-carved front door.

I'd once cleaned those windows. I'd planted flowers in that barrel. I'd rocked in one of those chairs and walked through that front door.

Katherine had been the one to pick Montana. She'd found us jobs at this guest ranch when Londyn and I had agreed to come along. The three of us had packed our meager belongings, bought bus tickets and waited for her to turn eighteen. Then we'd said goodbye to Karson, Clara, Aria and our beloved junkyard, setting out from California to Montana on a Greyhound bus because we'd craved adventure. Not for money or power or fame, but for an experience worth retelling.

We'd been so excited. So eager. We'd been so free.

No, not we. Me. I'd been excited and eager and free.

Somewhere along the way, that eighteen-year-old girl had gotten lost.

I parked the Cadillac in one of the guest spaces, not designated by a curb, but by an old-fashioned hitching post. My hands were suddenly like Jell-O and it took all my strength to shove the car in park.

Was it too late to turn around?

Yes.

I was here and damn it, I was doing this. With my eyes closed, I sucked in a calming breath and blew it out with an audible whoosh. When was the last time I'd been this nervous?

Leaning heavily into the door, I shoved it open. My purse stayed in the passenger seat because there was no such thing as petty theft at the Greer Ranch. The guests here didn't need to steal and I doubted any employee would dare cross the Greers—they were too well respected and that likely hadn't changed.

I swallowed down the lump in my throat and began the trek to the porch. My fingers gripped the wooden railing as my unsteady legs climbed the five stairs. Then with another shaky breath, I turned the knob on the door and walked inside.

The smell of cedar and cinnamon filled my nostrils. Someone had started a wood fire in the hearth. The couches surrounding the fireplace and rock chimney were the same chocolate leather. The plaid toss pillows looked new.

I tipped my chin to take in the vaulted ceiling's wooden beams. A wide, sweeping staircase ran to my right and another to my left, both the same wood color as the floor. Directly in front of me was the reception desk, currently unoccupied. And behind me, above the door, was a mounted, eight-point bull elk bust.

Clive.

Londyn, Katherine and I had affectionately named the elk Clive the month after we'd arrived. None of us had ever seen a taxidermic animal before Clive, and we'd thought he'd deserved a name.

I smiled, happy he was still here. Happy that, besides minor changes, this place hadn't changed.

It was like stepping back in time, to the days when my

younger self had two best friends and ambitions bigger than the sky.

This room hadn't changed.

But the woman standing in it sure had.

I walked to the counter, spying a silver service bell that hadn't been there before. I touched my finger to the plunger and the ding chorused through the room.

"One minute!" a voice called from the hallway that ran behind the staircase on my left. One minute was actually ten seconds. A flash of white hair caught my eye first as a woman emerged, drying her hands on a white towel.

"Morning." She smiled and my heart melted.

I'd missed that smile.

"Good morning," I said, praying she'd recognize me. Though I wouldn't fault her if she didn't. I'd only worked here for eight months, eleven years ago. The Greers had likely met a hundred seasonal workers since.

"What can I do for"—her head cocked to the side and her eyes widened—"Gemma?"

Thank God. She hadn't forgotten me. "Hi, Carol."

"Oh my word, Gemma!" She threw the towel on the reception desk and came right into my space, pulling me into a tight embrace. "My God, girl. How long has it been?"

"About eleven years." I laughed. "It's good to see you, Carol."

"Honey, you are just . . ." She let me go to look me up and down. "Stunning. Though you always were."

"And you are as beautiful as always."

"Please." She rolled her eyes. "I'm old."

The lines around Carol's eyes and mouth had deepened over the years but her hair was the same bright white, braided in a long, thick rope that draped over one shoulder. Her eyes were the same welcoming brown.

"What are you doing here?" she asked. "Where have you been all these years? Can you stay for dinner?"

I laughed, thinking that Benjamin would love Carol and her endless string of questions. "I've been living in Boston, but I'm on a vacation of sorts."

Permanently.

"Great." Carol's hands flew into the air, then she rushed around the side of the counter and began shaking a mouse to wake up a computer. "Do you want a king-size bed facing the valley? Or a queen with the mountain view?"

"Oh, no. That's okay. I've got a room in Missoula." It was forty miles away and the perfect excuse to leave before I wore out my welcome.

She ignored me. "King or queen?"

"Really, I don't need a room. I just wanted to swing by and see the place. If Katherine is still here, I'd, um . . . I'd love to say hello."

Understanding filled Carol's gaze and she nodded. The look wasn't harsh, and it didn't hold judgment, but she knew what I'd done to Katherine. She just wasn't holding it against me.

Carol might be the only one here who didn't.

"Yes, Katherine's here," she said. "She's in her office working. I'll take you up there after you tell me what room you want so I can have one of the boys haul up your luggage."

Maybe I'd known or hoped this would happen, because my luggage was packed in the Cadillac and I hadn't extended my reservation in Missoula. I'd just asked the clerk this morning if they had vacancies in case I returned.

"Queen, please." I wanted the mountain view. "My credit card is in my car."

"You're not paying," she said as she clicked and scrolled, eyes glued to the screen.

"I insist."

"Honey, I know it's been a lot of years but a smart girl like you, I'm sure you remember who's in charge around here."

I laughed. "Yes, ma'am."

"Better." She clicked one last time, then shoved the mouse aside.

Carol was in charge. She and her husband, Jake Sr., had started the Greer Ranch nearly fifty years ago. After their livestock operation had become successful, they'd expanded to start the resort, eventually passing it all down to their son, JR.

JR had been the manager of the entire operation when I'd worked here. Maybe he still was.

Or maybe Easton had taken over.

Regardless, Carol was in charge. She told the men exactly what she expected and heaven help them if they didn't follow orders.

Carol came around the counter and looped her arm through mine. "How did Boston treat you?"

"Quite well for a time."

"I can see that." She gave me another appraisal. "You always were classy. Even without a penny to pinch between your fingers, you had that air of sophistication about you. That air is still there, but I see you've got the pennies now too."

"I've saved a couple." My net worth was close to twenty million dollars. Yet standing beside Carol, I was the poor person in the room.

The land they owned in this gorgeous valley in Western Montana was worth hundreds of millions of dollars. Not that she'd flaunt it. That wasn't Carol's style. No, she was the woman with money in the bank and horse shit on her boots because a good day to her was working on this land.

I smiled and leaned in closer. "How is Jake?"

"Ornery." She shook her head. "That man hates being retired but he's so damn stubborn he won't admit it. So he putzes around, driving the rest of us who are trying to work crazy. Especially Easton. It's not a weekday if those two aren't fighting."

My heart skipped at the mention of his name. It had crossed my mind countless times on the drive here.

Easton Greer was another reason I'd stayed away. Another mistake. Someone I doubted would welcome me with open arms.

But this trip wasn't about him. I was going to find the courage to make things right with Katherine.

Any amends with Easton would be a bonus.

Maybe he'd forgotten all about me. In a way, I hoped he had.

Carol led me up the staircase, keeping a firm hold on my arm, as we made it to the first landing, rounded the corner and started up flight two. If she noticed my shaking fingers, she didn't show it.

"Katherine runs the resort side of things these days. We kept promoting her from job to job, and when we finally ran out of rungs on the ladder for her to climb, we just made her the boss."

"That doesn't surprise me in the least."

Katherine might not have had my bold ambition, but she'd always been smart and incredibly hardworking. Like me, she'd stopped going to school once she'd come to live in the junkyard. Instead, she'd worked. During the day, she'd had a job with a landscaping company. And at night, she'd washed dishes for a restaurant. Both had paid cash under the table.

The two of us had been more than friends. We'd been roommates. She'd shared my tent—though tent had never been the right word. It had started as a tent, with a tarp strung between two piles of junk to keep the rain away. Then I'd added sheet-metal walls and eventually separate bedrooms, one for me and another for Katherine. Our makeshift living room had become the common area for meals and games.

That tent had been my pride and joy, much like the empire I'd built in Boston.

An empire I'd built by leaving Katherine behind.

My shoes and Carol's boots echoed on the floor's wooden planks as we reached the second story and started down a long hallway, lined with doors.

I hadn't spent much time in this wing of the lodge since it was where the offices were located. The other wing was much larger and held all the guest rooms. I'd spent plenty of time in that wing as a housekeeper.

The Greer Ranch and Mountain Resort had become one of Montana's premier guest ranches, offering a *traditional western experience*. I'd done some googling in my hotel room last night and had been impressed by the website. The resort had always been nice, but over the past decade, they'd built five different chalets for guests to rent. They'd added more guest experiences and the meals were five-star. Prices weren't listed on the website because this place catered to celebrities and the uber-rich.

"Is she happy here?" I asked Carol.

She reached a door, rapped on it once with her knuckles.

"Come in," a voice I hadn't heard in years called from the other side.

My palms began to sweat.

Carol nodded for me to go on in. "Ask her yourself. I'll be downstairs in the kitchen. Come find me when you're ready to haul in your luggage."

"Okay," I breathed and turned the knob. *Here goes.* With my shoulders squared, I pushed the door open and took one step inside.

Katherine, beautiful as ever, sat behind a wide oak desk. She looked up from her computer screen and her entire body stiffened. "Gemma?"

"Hi." I lifted my hand for an awkward wave and braved another step.

Her eyebrows came together. "W-what are you doing here?"

"I came to see you." I sucked in some oxygen. *Breathe.* "May I?" I asked, coming into the room and motioning to one of the leather club chairs positioned in front of her desk.

She nodded but otherwise sat perfectly still in her high-backed chair.

Her corner office was enormous, as big as the one I'd had in Boston. The interior walls had floor-to-ceiling bookshelves and the others were lined with windows. A couch and two loveseats angled toward the view occupied half of the room.

It was classy yet comfortable. Inviting and clean. The

entire setup suited her completely.

Though Katherine had always fit here.

From the day we'd stepped off the bus, it had seemed like she'd found the place where she'd fit. Today, she looked even more at home, sitting at a fancy desk, wearing jeans and boots, with a picture window at her back and the mountains in the distance.

Her dark hair hung straight and sleek past her shoulders. Its natural shine was something I'd envied as a teenager—adult too. And I had yet to meet a person on earth with bluer eyes than Katherine Gates. They were almost exactly the color of the cloudless sky through the window.

She folded her hands together, leaning on the papers scattered on her desk. Her expression was neutral but there was a wariness in her gaze.

Katherine was six inches shorter than my five seven. She had a petite frame and trim figure. But sitting behind that desk, she was a force of her own. She was the boss and this was her throne.

It was a good look for her.

"How are you?" I asked.

"Good, thanks." Her tone was polite. Cautious. "You?"

"I'm good." I crossed my legs, trying to appear relaxed when I was the furthest thing from it. "Carol told me you're running the resort. Congratulations."

"Thank you."

The silence that followed was excruciating.

What felt like an hour was likely seconds, but the message was clear. Katherine didn't want me here, so I gave myself a mental shove to get this over with.

Sorry. That was all I had to say. I'm sorry.

So what the hell are you waiting for, Gemma?

"I wanted to—"

The phone on Katherine's desk rang. She pushed a button to shut it off, but not one second after it quieted, her cell phone began to vibrate. She silenced it too. "What were you saying?"

The confidence I'd summoned evaporated. The last thing I wanted was to fumble through this and risk coming across as hurried and insincere.

"I'm interrupting." I stood from the chair. "I'll let you get back to work. Maybe we could meet for coffee later."

"Today's crazy. I, um . . . maybe I could take a late lunch around one. But I'd only have thirty minutes."

I'd dodged many people with the late, short lunch before.

Which meant this was my chance to say my peace and then get the hell off the Greer Ranch.

I recognized when I wasn't welcome.

"It's okay." I gave her a sad smile. "Mostly, I just wanted to say that I'm sorry. You were my friend and how I left, what I did, it wasn't okay."

"Is that why you're here?"

"Yes."

Katherine stared at me, her expression unreadable.

Then slowly, it softened. Warmth spread into her eyes and her hands unclasped. "Are you staying?"

"If you don't mind." No matter what Carol said, if Katherine had a problem with me being here, I'd leave.

"No, I don't mind. I do have a crazy day. I was going to eat lunch at my desk. But maybe we could meet for dinner. In the dining room around six?"

"That would be wonderful." I let myself out, holding my smile until I was in the hallway. Then I let it stretch as years of regret and guilt vanished.

She doesn't hate me.

I could leave right this minute and feel like this trip had been valuable. But I wasn't going to leave. I was going to have dinner with my friend and hopefully rekindle a relationship I'd once held dear. My feet were practically floating as I descended the stairs.

Carol wasn't at the front desk, so I opted to head outside and collect my suitcase. I opened the door, a smile still on my face, and collided, headfirst, with a wall of muscle.

"Oh, sorry." I looked up and my heart stopped.

The smell of leather and aftershave filled my nose. I looked up to see a pair of dark brown eyes hooded by long, onyx lashes. I took in the straight nose, the sharp jaw and strong chin. My gaze dropped to the full lips I'd tasted once, on a night eleven years ago.

I'd never seen a face as symmetrical and so beautifully masculine as Easton Greer's.

Even when he scowled, like he was now, it was a wonder.

He'd gotten even more handsome. How was that possible? He'd transformed from a young man to just a man, man. Rugged and rough and sexy.

"Gemma." My name came out as a growl in his deep voice and I tore my gaze away from his mouth, taking a step back.

"Hi," I breathed, the air heavy and thick.

He took a step away, then another, his glare unwavering.

Easton cast his scowl over his shoulder and spotted the Cadillac. "That yours?"

"Yes."

"You're staying here." Not a question. An accusation. If he had it his way, I'd be uninvited.

I lifted my chin. "Yes, I came to see Katherine."

His jaw ticked. "I thought we'd gotten rid of you years ago."

Ouch. I guess he was still pissed about that whole sex in his room and waking up to find me gone.

But, good or bad, he hadn't forgotten me.

CHAPTER THREE

EASTON

What the fuck was she doing here?

I stormed through the wide, open barn door and kicked a clump of dirt. "And who the fuck is bringing dirt into my barn?"

I looked around, spotting a four-wheeler parked in the middle of the space that hadn't been there ten minutes ago. Its wheels were caked with mud. Someone—my grandfather—had probably been driving it around the lower meadow. We'd had a good rain last night and the ground was soggy.

Sure enough, Granddad emerged from behind the tractor at the far end of the building. He had a travel mug in one hand and a wrench in the other. "What's crawled up your ass this morning?"

"We just swept out this floor." I pointed to the four-wheeler. "Maybe next time you could park it outside. Save my crew from doing cleanup twice."

"It's a barn, Easton." He frowned. "And in my day, the crews didn't have much time to sweep."

My day. For fuck's sake. The last thing I needed this morning was a lecture about how this ranch had been run in his day.

I clenched my fists and kept my mouth shut before we got into a fight that would have my father playing mediator, my mother reminding me to have patience and Grandma lecturing me about respect.

The bottom line? I'd been put in charge of this ranch but Granddad hadn't read the memo.

He reminded me daily of how he'd done things in *my day.* He'd done the same to Dad when Dad had been running the show, though it had never bothered my father the way it irked me. Maybe because Dad and Granddad usually were of the same mind.

They both questioned my decisions. Yet we were thriving because I'd pushed and pushed and pushed to do things differently.

Neither of them had cared if the barn was clean. Granddad was right, he hadn't had staff to tidy up because both he and Dad had run with a skeleton crew for so damn long that we'd gotten the reputation for burning out ranch hands faster than we could hire their replacements.

According to Granddad, I'd overstaffed the ranch. But I liked to keep my guys for longer than one season. And I liked to have a clean barn, clean horses and clean equipment.

The tractor he'd been tinkering with had lasted seven years longer than any he'd had in his day. Maybe it was because he was a good mechanic. Or maybe it was because I had insisted on both servicing it *before* it broke down and keeping it inside, out of the elements.

"What are you doing?" I asked, looking over his shoulder to the John Deere.

"I'm checking the hydraulics on the tractor. If that's *all right* with you."

"Fine," I gritted out, turned and walked away.

I loved my grandfather, but damn it, working with the man was exhausting.

I couldn't assign him work. I couldn't hold him responsible for doing something on a regular basis because he was *retired*. And because Jake Greer Sr. reported to no one but his wife.

The problem was Granddad didn't want to be retired. He'd pop in and take over jobs while I was in the middle of them. He'd take work from one of my hands without letting me know. He'd give orders to my staff, sending them in the wrong direction, all because he was bored—something he'd never admit.

Like the hydraulics. I'd already planned on checking them this afternoon. He knew I was going to do it myself because I'd told him yesterday. But did he ask if there was something else I could use his help on? No.

I walked out of the barn and stalked to the stables, my sanctuary. It was twice as big as the barn, and everyone, even Granddad, knew this was my domain. The floors were swept out regularly and every horse's stall was mucked daily. We kept this place spotless, not only for the animals and my mental state, but because unlike the barn, guests roamed in here often.

As I made my way down the long center aisle, I counted the empty stalls. Most of the animals were out on guest excursions except for three young mares that had been left behind. They didn't spare me so much as a glance, too busy munching on the grain they'd been given this morning.

Above me, the lofts were full of bales and the florescent lights were shining bright. It smelled like all stables should in my opinion, of horses, hay and hard work.

My gelding Jigsaw popped his head out of his stall the moment he heard my boots on the cement floor. I walked to him, putting my hand on his cheek. "How do you feel about doing some work today?"

He nuzzled my shoulder, anxious to get outside.

Jigsaw had been my horse since I was eleven. He stood nearly sixteen hands and was a beast of an animal. He was fast and not afraid to work. He'd gotten his name from the puzzle-piece-shaped spot on his right shoulder. Besides that white mark, he was as black as the midnight sky.

I could always count on Jigsaw. He'd never let me

down. He never meddled with my schedule. He never talked back.

He never disappeared, only to return out of the blue eleven years later.

"What the fuck is she doing here?" I asked my horse.

He flicked up his nose, butting against my head.

"Yeah, we'll get going soon." I stroked the bridge of his nose and left him to get myself ready.

My office was located in the stables, beside the tack room. Dad had suggested I use the corner office in the lodge, the one opposite Katherine's, because more and more, I found myself behind a desk.

It would make things more efficient if I was sitting inside where I could talk to Katherine in person rather than call her twelve times a day. But I liked my cramped office in the stables. I liked that I could watch the trainers and the hands interact with the horses and the guests. I could witness who had the patience to take groups out on trail rides and who would be better suited for ranch maintenance.

And I liked working with the smell of horses and leather and dirt in the air.

But it meant when I needed to talk to Katherine, I had to call. When she didn't answer, I'd trek to the lodge for a cup of coffee and pop by her office.

Running into Gemma Lane had nearly knocked me on my ass.

I swiped my phone from my desk and shoved it into a

jeans pocket. Then I grabbed a pair of leather gloves from the top of a file cabinet and took my Stetson off the set of deer antlers I used as a hat hook. I needed to get out of here and get some air. Think this over.

"Hey, boss." Rory appeared in the doorway, bouncing from foot to foot.

"Hey." I put the hat on my head. "What's up?"

"I'm all done with the stalls for the day, and I'm ready to help on the tractor."

Rory was the son of one of our longtime housekeepers. As a single mom, she'd worked hard to provide for her son. He'd just turned eighteen and had graduated from high school this past spring. His mom's dream was for him to go to college. Rory's was to work on this ranch.

So I'd hired him. The kid soaked up everything we could teach him. He didn't bitch about the shit—literal—jobs. And if there was a chance for him to do something with the equipment, he was all over it.

I'd promised him yesterday he could shadow me as I worked on the tractor.

"Change of plan. Jake is working on the tractor today. He said he'd love to have your help."

"Okay, cool. Thanks."

"When you're done, take lunch. Then we'll wait for the trail rides to get back in. I'm going to check the fence on the south side. Just hang out and help the guys with the horses when they get back."

"Will do." He jogged out the door.

Rory jogged everywhere. His energy was impossible to contain and he always had a slew of questions.

Those questions would drive Granddad, a guy who preferred to work in silence, nuts.

I chuckled.

"What are you laughing about?" My brother, Cash, strode into the office.

"I sent Rory to help Granddad service the tractor."

He laughed too. "You'll pay for that later."

"Worth it." I grinned. "I thought Katherine had you out with the guests this morning."

"The folks staying in the Beartooth Chalet canceled their ride. They decided to hike up the ridge and take some pictures since the weather's good. We'll ride tomorrow."

I swiped another pair of gloves from the pile of my spares. "Good. Then you can help me."

"What are we doing?" he asked as I slapped the gloves into his chest and eased past him out the door.

"Fencing."

"I knew I should have gone to see Grandma instead of coming out here."

I walked to the wall where my saddle was draped over a thick wooden post. I pulled off a saddle blanket and grabbed a currycomb, then went to Jigsaw's stall. I'd planned on just taking a survey and noting damage today, but if Cash was free, we'd tackle the repairs too.

"Do you want to ride or take the truck?" I asked.

"I'll take the truck," he grumbled. "Since obviously you're going to ride."

I didn't feel bad for making Cash drive. He spent three times as long as I did on horseback, and he could be behind the wheel for a change.

It didn't take me long to get Jigsaw saddled and outside. The crisp fall air filled my lungs and he pranced on his feet, anxious to get out in the open. My horse loved to run, but he'd been trained to wait. When I left him standing in a spot, his reins not secured, he stood and waited.

Because he was a damn good horse.

Cash pulled up with the fencing truck, the blue Ford we kept stocked with a pile of steel fence posts and a roll of barbed wire. On a thirteen-thousand-acre ranch there was always fencing to do.

"Lead the way." He waved toward the two-wheel path that would take us to the south part of the ranch.

I mounted Jigsaw and clicked my tongue to walk away from the stables. When we hit grass, I gave him his head and let him go, our pace starting as an easy lope until he was galloping through the meadow.

My heart raced as the air whipped in my face. As he picked up speed, my muscles contracted, my core engaging and my thighs warming. I gave Jigsaw another nudge, letting him break to full throttle.

We were both panting when we hit the tree line. I

DEVNEY PERRY

slowed him down and turned, seeing Cash a way back, the truck bouncing through the middle of the field.

"Good boy." I patted Jigsaw's neck, his hide sweating. Then I wiped my own sweaty brow with my shirtsleeve.

The lodge stood tall and proud in the distance. I didn't spend much time there during the day—it had never felt as much like *my place* as the barn or stables—but it was mine.

I'd be avoiding that building like the damn plague since Gemma was somewhere inside.

Her face, shocked and beautiful, was burned into my brain. Those pink lips looked as soft as I remembered. Her hair was longer now, hanging in artful waves to the middle of her back. Her eyes were that same mesmerizing hazel.

She'd grown into a stunning woman.

Exactly what I didn't need on this ranch. I wasn't sure how long she'd planned to stay, but I had enough to deal with on a good day, with the regular ranch and resort workload. We were gearing up to begin winter prep. There was firewood to cut. The cows would need to be brought down to the meadows from where they'd spent their summer grazing in the mountains.

It was not the time to have an old fling show up at my damn front door.

I'd done a fine job of forgetting Gemma Lane.

At least, I thought I'd forgotten her. The knee-jerk reaction and the fact that now I couldn't *stop* thinking about her said otherwise.

She needed to go back to wherever she'd come from

and remember that she didn't belong here. Just like she hadn't belonged here years ago. With any luck, her visit would end before sundown.

Cash pulled up with the truck and rolled down his window. "You okay?"

"Yeah. Why?"

"You shot out of there like your heels were on fire."

"Just wanted to give Jigsaw a chance to run."

"Sure," he deadpanned. "You know, before I came to the stables, I helped this hot brunette with a kickass car haul her suitcase into the lodge. She looked awfully familiar, and you're in a lousier than normal mood today. She wouldn't have anything to do with it, would she?"

I gritted my teeth. "No."

He chuckled. "Whatever you say, brother."

Luggage. *Fuck.* She was staying.

How did Cash even remember Gemma? When she'd worked here before, he'd been away at college in Idaho. He must have remembered her from a trip home for spring break.

Meanwhile, I'd been here when Gemma, Kat and their other friend had arrived, having just graduated from Montana State. I'd been twenty-two, educated and energized with ideas for taking this ranch to the next level.

It had taken me over a decade to implement some of those ideas. Others had died along the way.

"I want to get through this pasture today if we can," I

told Cash, needing to concentrate on work for a few hours. "Hopefully it's not too bad."

"Sounds good. I rode out here last week with Kat so she could try out that mare. I didn't notice any wires down but we didn't ride down the line."

"Fingers crossed this won't take more than a day. I'd like to get the yearlings in here next week."

Cash's forehead furrowed. "Dad said we were going to use this as the calving pasture this year and the yearlings were going north of the highway."

"What? When?"

"Yesterday. Day before. I don't know. I assumed he told you."

"No," I snapped. "He didn't."

And goddamn it, that wasn't Dad's decision to make. Not anymore.

He'd agreed to let me handle the land. I had a degree in rangeland management and another in animal science. This pasture didn't have enough grass for all the pregnant cows, and we'd end up hauling hay. But it would be the perfect pasture to let the yearlings graze before we sold them in a few weeks.

"Son of a bitch."

"Don't shoot the messenger." Cash held up his hands. "I thought it was your idea."

No, it was not. Which meant I'd have to have another lengthy discussion—argument—with Dad this week. "Let's get to work."

Jigsaw didn't need any prompting to walk easily along the barbed wire fence. He sauntered slowly so I could inspect each of the five wires and make sure none were too loose or broken. When we reached a section where a post had begun to lean and tug the wires out of alignment, I dismounted and set it to rights before continuing down the line.

Damn it to hell.

I was pissed at Granddad for being himself. I was frustrated that Dad would never let go, like his father. And I was angry that ten seconds with Gemma had me so twisted up that when I passed a downed wire, Cash had to holler at me to stop.

"What's up with you?" he asked, getting out of the truck.

"Just got some shit on my mind."

"Let's hear it."

I looked at my brother as he crossed his arms and leaned on the grill of the truck. He wasn't going anywhere until I unloaded.

"I'm tired." I sighed. "Tired of not being heard." Tired of not feeling like I had some control over my own destiny.

"It's just habit, East. They aren't doing it to run you off, they just don't know any better. I mean, look how long it took Granddad to let Dad run the show. You were— what?—a senior when he retired? I was a sophomore."

"Maybe I should have taken over the resort when Grandma asked me to."

"Dealing with guests all day? Pampering them? You would have hated that job. Besides, Katherine is perfect for it."

She was exactly the right person for that job and everyone knew it, including me. Which was why no one challenged Katherine. When she had an idea, everyone was all ears.

Maybe that was because the resort side of the business had always been Grandma's passion. When she had announced that she wanted to start a resort and was using five million dollars to build the lodge, Granddad had stayed quiet and smiled as she'd written the first check.

That was when the resort had been a hobby. A side gig. I always thought Granddad had believed in Grandma, but he hadn't expected it to take off. He certainly hadn't imagined it would ever be as successful as it was today.

The resort was pulling in more and more income each year, and Katherine had more freedom to run the business than I'd ever had managing the ranch. And I'd lived here my entire life.

"They listen to her," I said. "Completely. It's hard not to get jealous."

"And it's hard not to get jealous when you weren't even in the running to take over the resort or the ranch."

Ah, hell. "Sorry."

I didn't mean to make Cash feel like a lesser contributor. I was tired of fighting with Dad and Granddad and I clearly forgot to keep my brother's feelings in check, especially with how much I valued his opinions.

"It's okay." Cash shrugged. "Things are better this way. I love my job and what I'm doing here. As long as I have my horses, I'm a happy man."

Soon he'd have more than just horses.

I hadn't told him or anyone yet, but I'd put in an offer to buy a patch of land bordering us on the west. If it came together, I was going to build another stable and ask Cash to take over as manager for a top-of-the-line equine breeding and training facility.

Cash had a gift when it came to horses and assessing their nature. It was time to put it to use. His talents were wasted catering to guests.

I prayed the purchase didn't fall through.

Or that my family found out and put a stop to something before I'd even gotten it started.

"Let's get this fixed." I jerked my chin to the fence.

Thirty minutes later, the section was fixed and we were moving down the line. As the hours passed, the tension in my shoulders eased. There was something comforting about physical labor that soothed my soul. Something relaxing about being on a horse.

It was in my blood. Working here called to my soul.

Cash was right about Dad and Granddad. They loved this work too. They didn't challenge me to be malicious, but they acted out of habit and because they were stubborn.

So was I.

It was a trait famously passed through the Greer bloodline. And while I could rationalize it in my head, it still annoyed me on the day-to-day.

By lunch, we'd finished checking the pasture's fence and my stomach was growling. I gave Cash a nod to head on back to the barn while Jigsaw and I made the return trip at an easier pace.

Most of my frustration from my family had worked its way out. Now it was mostly Gemma plaguing my mind.

Why was she here? How long was she staying? No matter the duration, I'd make sure to keep myself busy. There was no reason to see her except . . .

Shit. My family had loved Gemma, especially Grandma.

When she'd worked here, they'd been some of our first employees. Grandma had hired them after a phone interview with Katherine because she'd *liked the girl's spirit.*

Grandma didn't hire much anymore, but she'd always been a good judge of character.

And when three young women had arrived at the lodge, fresh faced and excited, Grandma had taken them under her wing. To this day, Grandma believed that was the best hiring decision she'd ever made.

Those three had cleaned, washed laundry, gardened and waitressed. Any job they were given, they did without question while wearing real smiles.

The first time I'd seen Gemma, she'd been polishing

silverware in the kitchen. I'd walked in, expecting it to be empty, but there she was, sitting on the stainless-steel table, rubbing a rag over a knife until she could see her reflection in the metal.

She'd flashed me a smile, hopped down and stuck out her hand.

I'd almost fallen over at that smile.

Then I'd done what all arrogant and stupid twenty-two-year-old guys did when faced with a gorgeous woman. I'd played it cool and ignored her. I'd pretended like I hadn't had the biggest crush of my life.

That had backfired spectacularly.

Because Gemma hadn't craved my attention. She'd been a force of her own, so tied up in her own life that others were forgotten.

What she'd done to Katherine was the perfect example.

And what she'd done to me.

Things were different now. I wasn't a young man driven by hormones and lust who wanted a young woman. Ignoring Gemma wouldn't be some tactic to woo her into my bed. I'd ignore her because sooner than later, she'd be gone anyway. I just had to bide my time for a week, maybe two.

Then Gemma Lane would disappear.

And I'd go back to forgetting the breathtaking woman with the sparkling hazel eyes who, turns out, I hadn't forgotten about, after all.

CHAPTER FOUR

GEMMA

"So basically, you quit your life?"

"Well, when you say it like that it makes me sound crazy."

"Wow." Katherine grabbed the bottle of wine from the middle of the table and topped off my glass. "How many days ago was this?"

"I left Londyn's a week ago. I left Boston a couple days before that."

"And here you are."

"Here I am."

I was sitting across from Katherine in the dining room at the lodge. We were sharing a piece of chocolate cheesecake, polishing off a bottle of wine, after we'd eaten a delicious dinner of roasted chicken and mashed potatoes. Their website had not exaggerated the quality of the food. Or the wine selection.

"How is Londyn?" Katherine asked.

"She's wonderful." I smiled. "She's married and has a baby girl. She's happy."

"I'm glad. I think about her, about everyone, from time to time."

"Even me?"

"Yes. But I was hurt when you left."

"I'm sorry." I'd keep apologizing until she forgave me. Or maybe until I forgave myself.

"Don't be." She gave me a sad smile. "It was about a year after you left, I was out riding with Carol one day, and I realized that this was where I'm supposed to be. I'm happy here. I love my job and the ranch and the Greers. They've kind of made me an honorary member of the family, and I couldn't have asked for better."

"I'm glad. And I'm still sorry."

"You're forgiven."

"Really? You're not going to make me work harder for it?"

She shrugged. "It's not my style."

No, it wasn't. Katherine was too honest and real to punish me for something she'd already let go. Even after all the shit she'd been dragged through, she had never turned bitter.

"It worked out how it should have," she said. "I would have gone with you to Boston and resented every second. At the time, the promise of all that money sounded so good. But the city isn't me. Real estate isn't me. I helped with one of the deals when the Greers were buying some acreage a few years ago and I hated every second. Talk about stress. And paperwork."

I laughed. "It's not without challenges."

"Did you enjoy it?"

"I did for a time. Mostly, it was the springboard." I'd used the money I'd made to invest in other venues.

Four months after we'd come to work at the Greer Ranch, Londyn had decided to try something new. She'd enjoyed Montana but it hadn't been her landing spot. She'd asked me to come with her, to head east, but I'd stayed behind with Katherine.

I'd liked working here and being one of those honorary Greer family members.

Then about four months later, Katherine and I had been working in this very dining room. She waitressed while I'd tended bar, filling in for one of the seasonal workers who'd quit to return home. A couple had come in for a nightcap and like all other guests here, they'd oozed money.

It had been an oddly quiet night and the room had cleared out earlier than normal. But the couple had stayed and visited with Katherine and me. Three hours later, we'd confided in them—something we *never* did—telling them the story of our childhood.

They'd found it tragically fascinating.

And that night, Sandra and Eric Sheldon had changed my life.

They owned a real estate company in Boston, brokering some of the finest homes in the city. Before they'd checked out of the resort, they'd offered both Katherine and me jobs. They'd offered to hire us at their firm and give us a shot.

Sandra had given us her business card and had asked that we consider the offer. That if we were interested, Boston was waiting and so was she.

It had been a once-in-a-lifetime opportunity.

I'd been ready to hop on the bus the next morning. Katherine had been more hesitant, not wanting to abandon the Greers until they'd had replacements hired.

The more she'd hesitated, the more anxious I'd been that the Sheldons would forget about us. That this chance to make it rich would evaporate.

As an ambitious nineteen-year-old, patience had not been a strength.

I'd craved adventure. I'd craved the promise of money, to become a woman like Sandra who wore jewels dripping from her ears and nails that would never be caked with dirt.

Katherine had begged me to wait and give our notice to the Greers together.

Two days later, without telling Katherine, I'd taken the Sheldons' card, packed up my things while she was cleaning a guest room and left. When I'd arrived in Boston and called Sandra, I'd lied and said that Katherine hadn't been interested.

When really, I'd left her behind.

I hadn't even written a note.

Because Katherine had known exactly where I'd gone. It was truly a miracle that she didn't hate me.

Over dinner tonight, I told her all about my life in Boston. How I'd worked as Sandra's assistant for six months until I had my license. How within two years, I'd become their highest grossing agent, specializing in elite Boston properties.

When real estate had become tedious, I'd started investing. Until one day, I hadn't needed to sell properties to survive. I'd laid the foundation of my empire and kept adding bricks.

I'd spent years trying to fill the hole in my chest with money and business. But even with all the power, the prestige, the fortune, that hole was still there.

The numbness remained.

I was still just a runaway kid, numb to the world, searching for anything to make her *feel*.

"Do you talk to anyone else?" Katherine asked. "From Lou's?"

"No, just Londyn. Do you?"

"No." She shook her head. "How did you know I was here?"

"A while back, I was curious where everyone had landed, so I hired an investigator to find out. You made his job easy since your picture was all over the resort's website."

"Ah. That makes sense."

"Did you hear that Lou died?"

"He did?" Her hand pressed against her heart. "How? When?"

"Years ago. He died in his sleep."

Tears shone in her blue eyes. "I'll never forget that man."

Lou Miley had owned the junkyard when Karson had discovered it after running away from home. Karson had snuck in and out for a month, sleeping there and hiding out, until one night, Lou had come out with a blanket.

Lou hadn't tossed Karson out. He hadn't brought him inside, either. He'd simply let Karson stay.

When I'd found Karson after leaving my own home, Lou hadn't even batted an eyelash the first time he'd spotted me in his junkyard. He'd given me a grunt and a glare and disappeared into the shack he'd called home.

"He was so grumpy." I smiled. "So wonderfully gruff and grumpy."

Lou had shunned the mainstream world, living alone at the junkyard. None of us had ever asked why he'd let six kids squat on his property, but I believed it was because when we'd moved in, Lou hadn't been so alone.

None of us, not even Karson, had ever been invited into Lou's home. But he'd allowed us to use the bathroom and the shower in the junkyard's shop. Once, Karson and I had been sick with a cold and Lou had left us a bottle of cold medicine by the sink.

Lou hadn't reported us as runaways. Most adults would have called the cops and ushered us into the foster care system. But I think Lou had liked having us there. And maybe he'd known that if he kicked us out or called the authorities, we would have just run away again, probably to a place not nearly as safe.

Returning home had not been an option for any of us.

"He saved us," Katherine whispered. "No one around here understands that, but Lou saved our lives."

"Yes, he did. I wish I would have gone to his funeral. The timing . . . it didn't work out." More like I hadn't made the time. "Do the Greers know? About our childhood?"

"Have you met Carol? She got me to blurt the whole thing one night about a month after you left. I was feeling alone and angry, so I told her everything. And there's no such thing as a secret on this ranch. The next night, I went to the family dinner and you should have seen all the pitiful looks. I was so pissed."

Which meant Easton knew too.

I'd kept my past to myself when I'd worked here. We all had. The Sheldons were the only people we'd told. At the time, I wasn't sure what had caused Katherine and me to spill our tale, to guests, no less. But after working with Sandra and Eric for a few years, I'd learned that it was their nature. They had this magnetic pull, a way of drawing people out of their shells.

Even after I'd stopped working for their firm, I'd kept

in touch with my former mentors. Sandra was my constant companion at Fashion Week in Paris.

There were others who knew my story—I'd spent years telling Dr. Brewer the horrid details—but the list was small. Not even Benjamin knew about my past. Because, as Katherine had said, the fastest way to earn someone's pity was to tell them about our youth.

I didn't want pity from the Greers. I certainly didn't want pity from Easton.

All I'd ever wanted from him was affection.

Which I'd gotten one glorious night.

Hours before I'd boarded a Greyhound bus and left Montana behind.

"Do you ever miss the tent?" Katherine asked, pouring us both more wine.

I laughed. "I don't miss sleeping on the ground, but I do miss the nights when we'd have everyone crowded inside because it was raining. I miss the days when we were all bored and would play cards for hours and talk and laugh."

"Me too. It's sad that we've all lost touch. But for me, it's easier this way. To just go on with my life and not look back. I mean, we were happy in the junkyard. As happy as homeless kids could be, but it was hard."

"So hard," I agreed. "My God, we were tough."

"And lucky."

There were countless other stories of runaway kids whose lives had been cut short. Whose lives had no happy ending. Kids who'd gotten addicted to drugs and alcohol. Girls who'd disappeared into a trafficking ring, never to be seen again.

Lucky was an understatement.

"I'm glad you came back," Katherine said. "It's good to see you."

"I'm glad I came too." There was a sense of peace here. A calm weight to the air. "It's relaxing."

"Tonight's a quiet night. You came at exactly the right time. Normally, the dining room is full until eight or nine. But this is a slow week."

Which explained why we were the only two in the room except some staffers wandering in and out, checking to see if Katherine needed anything.

After I'd settled into my guest room earlier, I'd called to check in with Benjamin. As expected, he had everything handled and no emergencies to report. But with nothing else to do—something that hadn't bothered me while I'd been driving *because* I'd been driving—I'd pulled out my laptop and spent an hour going through emails.

It had felt good to reconnect with that familiar part of me. The person who worked efficiently and effectively, checking boxes off lists and moving things forward.

Except there hadn't been much to move along. Mostly, it had been correspondence from my financial management team who were still processing the details from my sale of Gemma Lane. Then there'd been a few notes from acquaintances around Boston wondering if the rumors of my hastened exit from the city were true.

Those emails I'd simply deleted. There'd be buzz about my departure for weeks. People would speculate that I'd lost my mind or burned out. They'd gossip about my shortcomings or that the pressure had become too much.

It didn't matter.

Boston was history and I had no plans to return.

The rest of my afternoon had been spent reading. I couldn't remember the last time I'd read a book for sheer pleasure. I hadn't even owned a book, but my room had compensated for my shortcomings. It had come stocked with three different paperbacks in the dresser drawer.

I'd lost myself in a thriller until Katherine had knocked on my door around six for dinner. We'd been talking for hours. I'd told Katherine about my life and she'd told me about hers here at the resort.

My gaze traveled around the room in a slow, appraising circle. The tables were arranged much like a restaurant, in varying sizes, around the space. Katherine had explained that they employed a full-time chef and served both breakfast and dinner here. Sack lunches were available by request, mostly because keeping regular hours with the resort activities was difficult.

A few guests had come down for dinner but had since retired to their rooms. Others must have opted for room service. The guests who rented the chalets—at four thousand dollars per night—had access to a different chef who'd go to their chalets and prepare a private meal.

"This place looks fantastic," I told Katherine. "When I came in this morning, my first thought was how nothing here had changed. But that's not true, is it?"

"About four years ago, we started doing some renovations," she said. "Mostly cosmetic. Paint. Curtains. Art. Bedding. It's made a difference."

"It was your idea, wasn't it?"

She hid her smile in her wine.

The differences had Katherine's gentle and classic touch written all over them. She'd transformed the resort from lovely to magical.

The subtle differences had escaped my quick inspection earlier. The walls were a brighter shade of white, something that complemented the rich wood ceilings and floors. The chairs in the dining room had once been wooden, but they'd been replaced with cream upholstered pieces that softened the room and brightened the crystal chandelier's golden light.

It was still rustic, but now there was a chic edge to the decor. It was fancy without being pretentious but would appeal to the wealthy who could afford a vacation here.

"We actually did updates all over the ranch. The stables are a dream these days. You could eat off the floor because Easton insists on keeping them spotless."

Easton.

I'd seen him earlier from the window in my room.

He'd been riding a huge black horse through a meadow in the distance. I'd spied on him until he and his horse had become nothing but a fleck in the green pasture.

But I'd known it was him. I'd recognize Easton's broad shoulders and black cowboy hat anywhere. I remembered how his dark hair looked when the ends curled at the nape of his neck, and how his strong arms filled out the sleeves of his plaid, pearl-snap shirts.

The thud of boots echoed through the room, drawing me from my musings.

Katherine's attention darted over my shoulder. "Hey."

"Hey."

Tingles ran up my spine at the familiar deep rumble.

But I refused to turn and pay Easton any mind. He'd been cold and unfriendly to me for as long as I could remember. Well, except that one night. But after today's collision by the front door, it seemed nothing had changed.

"What's up?" Katherine asked him.

"Came to grab some dinner before I go home."

Home? It was almost nine o'clock at night. Didn't he have a wife or a girlfriend waiting?

"You remember Gemma, don't you?" Katherine gestured to me with her wineglass.

I looked over my shoulder and gave him a tight smile.

Easton was standing at my side, his arms crossed over his chest. His jaw was granite and his eyes didn't so much as flicker my direction.

He ignored Katherine's reintroduction entirely.

Asshole. "Nice to see you again, Easton. You look . . . older."

Older. Sexy as hell. *Same thing.*

He harrumphed, but didn't bother with any other acknowledgement, addressing only Katherine as he spoke. "I need an hour tomorrow when you have one to go over some schedules. I need to steal a couple of the hands from guest services to help move some steers."

"Okay." She nodded. "I'll check my calendar and shoot you a text with the time."

"Fine."

"Would you like to join us?" She gestured to the empty seat beside me.

Easton answered by walking out of the room, not sparing me another glance before he disappeared through the door that led to the kitchen.

Wow.

"I see you two still hate each other."

It had never been hatred. More like two kids who hadn't realized that hate was actually foreplay.

Katherine stood from her chair and walked over to the bar along the rear wall. She swiped a wine bottle off the shelf, opened it with the corkscrew and brought it to the table. "I'll probably regret this bottle in the morning."

"Me too." I held up my glass.

"How long are you staying?"

"I don't know. A day or two. Is that okay? If you have an incoming reservation, I can take off tomorrow."

"No, stay. I'll need the room back next week. It's hunting season and we're booked solid through Christmas. But if you want to stay longer, you can stay at my place. We have a guest bedroom that's always empty."

"We?" My eyes darted to her naked ring finger. "I didn't know you were living with someone."

"I live with Cash."

"Oh. I didn't realize you were together."

"No, no, no." She waved it off. "We're not together. We're just roommates. And coworkers. And friends."

Friends. With the way she stressed the word, either he wanted more, and she wasn't interested, or it was the other way around.

Cash had been at college when I'd worked here, and I'd only spoken to him once when he'd come home for spring break. But I'd recognized him instantly when he'd helped me bring my luggage into the lodge earlier. He had the same good looks as his older brother, though Easton carried a rougher edge. The biggest difference between the Greer men was that Cash was nice.

Easton, not so much. Though he was nice to look at.

"Carol and Jake built a house in the foothills about five years ago," Katherine said. "Cash and Easton were living in their old place, but a few years ago, Easton decided to build too. So rather than stay in one of the staff apartments, it made sense for me to move into the house. It was getting weird for the staffers to have the boss living next door."

The staff quarters were what I'd imagined a college dorm was like. Fun for a younger crowd but totally impractical for adults who'd outgrown their communal living days.

I'd loved living in the quarters. I'd loved having a decent shower and soft mattress. The accommodations weren't spacious, but for Katherine, Londyn and me, they'd been sublime. A giant step up from the junkyard.

The door to the kitchen opened and Easton came striding out carrying a plate covered with aluminum foil in his hand. He kept his brown eyes aimed forward, not oblivious to the way Katherine and I watched him walk, just uncaring.

Was he heading to his house alone? Even with the foil, I could tell his plate was heaped with food. It was enough for two people.

There was no chance Easton was still single. He was an extremely sexy man with a steady job and an ass that looked delicious in a pair of Wranglers.

And without.

Too bad he was a jerk and probably married. A night with Easton Greer was exactly the thing my newly spontaneous self would have applauded.

"Goodnight," Katherine called to his back as he walked past the threshold that connected the dining room to the lobby.

Easton's steps didn't slow. "Night, Kat."

Rejected again. *Damn.* Eleven years later and it stung.

But there was no use dwelling on the actions of a man I'd leave behind in a day or two. I'd done that enough. I'd wished for his warm smile when all I'd ever received was the cold shoulder.

That hadn't changed. The only time he'd taken notice was the night I'd let him take me to his bed.

A night I hoped had remained a secret.

"He calls you Kat?" I asked.

"It's something Cash started." She shrugged. "I'm the little sister, so I got a nickname."

A nickname and status she didn't want. At least, not with Cash. Her *friends* comment was beginning to make sense.

"Would you like to go on a few excursions while you're here? Maybe a ride or a hike while the weather's good?" she asked, changing the subject.

I hummed, sipping my wine and thinking it over. Without work, I had nothing to do but sit in my room. "I haven't ridden a horse since I was here last. That might be fun."

"Great. I'll arrange a private lesson for you tomorrow."

"Perfect." When she raised her glass, I clinked mine to hers. "There's something else I wanted to talk to you about. Carol wouldn't let me pay when I checked in, but I'd like to. Can you make that happen? Please? She did so much for me, and the least I can do is pay for my room."

"If she finds out, I'm dead meat."

I zipped my lips shut.

"Okay." She laughed. "You can pay."

"Thanks." I smiled. "And thanks for hearing me out. I know I've said it about a hundred times tonight, but I am sorry. Truly."

"It's okay, Gemma."

"Are you sure?"

Katherine nodded. "I swear. It's forgotten."

The two of us stayed in the dining room until midnight, chatting and drinking more wine before saying our goodnights. When I fell asleep, it was with a smile and a light heart.

Katherine didn't hate me. She'd accepted my apology. And I'd reunited with my friend.

But the next morning when I showed up at the stables for my riding lesson, I realized I'd assumed too much. Maybe she was out to punish me for my mistake, after all.

Because Katherine, *my friend*, had paired me with the worst riding instructor on earth.

Easton.

"Forgotten, my ass," I muttered. "She hates me."

CHAPTER FIVE

EASTON

"What the fuck? *You're* my ten o'clock?"

"Hey, don't look at me like that." Gemma fisted her hands on her hips. "This wasn't my idea."

"Goddamn it." I pulled my phone from my pocket and called Kat's cell. She didn't answer. So I called her office. It went straight to voicemail. *Shit.* "I don't have time for this. We have paying customers who need lessons. And I have work to do."

"I am paying," Gemma shot back. "But forget it. I don't need to ride a horse this bad."

As she spun on a boot heel and marched away, my phone dinged with a text from Katherine.

EVERYONE ELSE WAS BOOKED. You were the only instructor available.

. . .

A MISTAKE I'd fix on next month's schedule.

Every month, Katherine and I sat down and outlined lesson blocks and paired them with instructors. We always made sure there was one private lesson slot available for one-on-one rides throughout the day because guests often had last-minute requests. So one instructor stayed behind, while the rest were sent out on the scheduled rides and lessons.

Personally, I hated the group shit. It was tedious and slow. I did better one-on-one when I could go wherever I wanted and the pace was faster. So when we were short-handed, like we were this week because one of the guys was on vacation, I was the backup for private lessons.

Starting tomorrow, I'd start training Rory so I'd never be on the damn schedule again.

My phone dinged again with another text from Kat.

SHE'S MY FRIEND. And a guest. Be nice. For me? Please?

YEAH, that's a no.

I loved Katherine. She'd melded into our family seamlessly and was the closest thing to a younger sister I'd ever have. She was hardworking, smart and kind. But adopted sister or not, there was no way in hell I was spending two hours alone with Gemma.

My phone buzzed again.

DO this lesson and I'll make sure Jake is too busy to bother you for two weeks.

KATHERINE WOULD PROBABLY beg Granddad with those blue eyes for a special task. Something that would flatter him and make him brag at family dinners. I could hear him already.

I can't help with the equipment next week. Katherine needs me.

Goddamn it. Younger sisters were overrated.

"Fine," I muttered, not bothering to respond. Kat knew she was dangling a carrot and I wouldn't resist.

"Wait," I called to Gemma's back as she neared the door.

She kept walking.

I tucked my phone away and chased after her, my long strides eating up the distance between us. "Gemma."

She didn't slow.

"Gemma!" I bellowed as she stepped out the door and into the sunshine. "Would you stop?"

"Why?" She spun around and threw her arms in the air. Her long ponytail whipped over her shoulder. "What now?"

I wasn't going to apologize or beg her to come back. Even two weeks without Granddad bothering me wasn't worth my pride. "Have you been on a horse in the past decade?"

"No. Hence the lesson."

My gaze traveled up and down her body. She was wearing an oatmeal sweater with a V-neck that dipped low enough to show the swell of her breasts and a pair of jeans that encased her toned thighs. They were cuffed at the ankle, above the line of her tan, suede boots. Her legs looked a mile long and behind my zipper, my dick stirred.

Christ. This lesson would be impossible if I couldn't keep my eyes off her.

"We're riding horses, not walking the runway," I snapped. "Do you have boots?"

"These are boots." Her eyes dropped to her feet. "What's wrong with them?"

"Those are *not* boots."

"They'll work for today." She crossed her arms over her chest.

"Don't come crying to me if you step in horse shit."

Her eyes narrowed. "I'll be fine."

Maybe if I pissed her off enough, she'd quit. Then I could tell Kat I'd held up my end of the bargain.

I turned and walked back inside, heading straight for Jigsaw's stall. I'd saddled him when Katherine had texted me about this *last-minute lesson*. She hadn't bothered to give me the client's name. Another mistake. If I couldn't avoid the schedule, I'd ask for specifics from now on.

"Come on, boy." I hadn't bridled him yet, so I took his halter and led him into the arena beside the stables. When I went back to get Gemma's horse ready, I'd hoped she might have changed her mind.

But no. She was standing beside Sprite's stall, stroking the mare's cheek. I'd planned on taking Pepsi, one of our other mares and Sprite's sister, but when a rider took a shine to a horse and that affection seemed to go both ways, sometimes it was best to go with it.

"That's Sprite."

"Hi, Sprite." She smiled at the horse's gray-speckled nose, her voice dropping to a sweet caress.

There'd been a time once when she'd given me that smile and talked to me with that same voice. The combination was a gut-puncher. But I refused to be jealous of a horse.

I yanked a currycomb off a peg beside the stall and nudged Gemma out of the way with my shoulder. The right thing to do would be to make her saddle Sprite, but that would involve a lot of close contact.

One of the other instructors could teach the woman how to strap on a saddle.

Not that I expected her to be here much longer anyway.

"When are you leaving?" I asked, sliding into the stall.

"Please tell me you're nicer to other guests."

I grunted and ran the comb over Sprite's back as she hovered by the horse's nose.

Actually, I was great with guests, not that I owed her an explanation. I wasn't charming like Katherine or charismatic like Cash, but I had my own appeal. Guests loved that I was authentic. I was a Montana rancher who loved the land, my family and a marbled, medium-rare steak.

They liked me because I loved my roots. Something Gemma wouldn't understand.

Gemma Lane was too wild for roots.

She'd run from here sooner than later, and this time, I wouldn't let it wreck me.

I wasn't sure where she'd been these past eleven years and I wasn't asking. Clearly, she'd run into some money. One look at her clothes and that Cadillac and you knew she had cash. If she was a paying guest, she'd come here to spend it.

"I don't know when I'm leaving," she said. "I don't really have a schedule."

"What about your job? Don't you need to get back to it?"

"I'm unemployed at the moment."

"I thought you left here to be some hotshot real estate agent."

"I was in real estate for a while. Then I invested in some other companies around Boston. Eventually I started a cosmetics company. I sold it three weeks ago so . . . unemployed."

"You made a couple bucks and decided to quit on payday." I scoffed. "Typical."

That was exactly what she'd done here. Gemma had earned a good wage, but when the promise of something more came along, she'd bailed, leaving her best friend behind in tears. And showing me exactly what she'd wanted from me—a roll between the sheets and a couple orgasms—nothing more.

Gemma's glare was waiting when I came out of the stall. "If you call twelve million dollars a couple of bucks, then yes. I quit on payday."

My feet faltered a step at the number.

She saw it. The corner of her mouth turned up as I marched past her to put the comb away and grab a saddle blanket.

Twelve million dollars was quite an accomplishment for a kid who'd lived in a junkyard, not that I'd give her anything resembling a compliment.

Katherine had told us about her homelife as a kid. How she'd run away from home, scared and hopeless, until some other kids had pulled her into their fold—Gemma being one of them.

They'd lived in a junkyard, for fuck's sake. Gemma and Katherine had built a tent out of sheet metal, tarps and whatever else they could find and had slept on the ground for years.

My horse lived better than that.

But looking at Gemma, you'd never know it. She held her shoulders straight. She kept her chin up. She was as shiny as my Sunday boots, and as refined as any of the wealthy people who shelled out thousands of dollars to go glamping here each summer.

And damn it, there was a swell of pride in my chest. *Twelve million dollars.* She'd made it. She'd set herself up to never sleep on the ground again.

"Why does it bother you that I'm here?" she asked as I came back with the saddle blanket.

"Because," I muttered.

Because she was a distraction. Because when she was here, I couldn't think straight. Because those hazel eyes were so enchanting, and if I let myself, I'd get swept up in her all over again.

She'd be gone soon, chasing the next dollar or wild adventure, leaving me behind, wondering what kind of man could compel her to stay.

It sure as fuck wasn't me.

We didn't speak as I finished saddling Sprite. She followed close behind when I led the horse out of her stall and to the arena, stopping inside the gate.

"Walk her in a circle to get her blood flowing."

"Okay." Gemma nodded, taking the leather straps in

her dainty hands. Her glossy nails caught the morning sun and they gleamed, clean and pale pink.

Mine were permanently stained with dirt.

As she walked Sprite, I hurried to my office and grabbed my hat. Then I scribbled a note for Rory to oil Mom's saddle before lunch. He was over at the barn, cleaning up the mess Granddad had brought in with the four-wheeler yesterday and the tools he hadn't put away.

If I made it through this lesson with Gemma, I'd have two weeks without Granddad screwing with my plans.

Theoretically.

Katherine was good at managing Granddad but she wasn't infallible. And he was unpredictable. But Sprite was saddled and so was Jigsaw, so I was committed to see this through.

With a deep breath, I returned to the arena. Private lessons were typically two hours, but this was going to be ninety minutes, max.

Gemma didn't hear me as I walked up. Sprite's hooves thudded in the soft dirt as Gemma led her in a circle, the noise drowning out the sound of my own footsteps.

"Okay, Sprite," Gemma said. "Help me out today. Don't make me look like a total fool in front of him. Please."

I froze. The way she'd pleaded with the animal, the vulnerability in her voice . . . *fuck*. She did a hell of a job making sure to keep her confidence in place, but to hear her beg a horse. Maybe it wasn't as steely as she pretended.

And maybe I was being a dickhead, punishing her for a decade-old mistake.

Jigsaw, the bastard, chose that moment to snort and caught Gemma's attention. When she spotted me listening in, the gentle expression she'd had with Sprite hardened.

"That's good enough." I closed the gap and tightened Sprite's cinch. Then I jerked my chin for Gemma to follow me to the horse's left side where I held the stirrup for her. "Foot in. Hand on the horn. Then up you go."

With one graceful swing, she was in the saddle. A small smile toyed on her pink lips.

I adjusted her stirrups, then handed her the reins. "Wait here."

Jigsaw jittered as I approached, the excitement radiating off his large body. "It's not that kind of trip today."

He nudged me in the shoulder with his nose, leaving a snot mark. "Thanks."

After a couple of walking laps, I cinched him up, pulled on his bridle and climbed on. I clicked my tongue and led the way out of the arena, heading toward the two-lane road that created a large loop in one of the pastures.

Sprite had been trained well. She followed behind Jigsaw without Gemma having to do a thing but stay seated.

I looked over my shoulder occasionally to check that Gemma was sitting correctly and wasn't choking up on the reins. Every time, I expected to make a correction but she looked good there. Natural.

"Come on up here." I pointed to the other lane. Having her behind me wasn't going to teach her anything about leading a horse if she was only following.

She nodded, her eyes fixed on Sprite's white mane, then gave a gentle nudge with her heels and steered to the right. When we were walking side by side, she glanced over.

Normally, this would be the time in a lesson when I'd shower a student with praise. *Good job, you steered the horse three feet to the right.* I'd prattle on about horses and gauge the student's comfort. I'd talk about the ranch and answer questions, making small talk and ensuring the student had a nice time.

Except this was Gemma. My normal approach had flown out the window when I'd snapped at her in the stables. And as much as I'd like a quiet, no-conversation ride, it actually made the tension worse.

"So you drove here?" I asked at the same time she said, "Katherine said you built a house."

"Uh . . . yeah," I answered. "A few years ago."

"I bet it's nice to have your own space. And yes, I drove here."

"Nice car."

"It's not mine. Do you remember Londyn?"

I nodded, recalling the blonde who'd arrived with

Gemma and Kat. She'd left not long after the first snow-storm. "The other friend."

"The Cadillac is hers. When we lived in the junkyard, it was her home, for lack of a better term. A while ago, she had it hauled from California to Boston and completely restored."

"How'd you end up with it?" Maybe she'd bought it with some of her millions.

"Londyn was driving it back to California a little over a year ago. She got a flat tire and ended up stuck in West Virginia. The mechanic who rescued her is now her husband. After I sold the company, I went to visit, and she got this crazy idea for me to take the car to California in her place."

Like I'd suspected, this was only just a temporary stop. "Why California?"

"To find an old friend from the junkyard. It was their car, Londyn and Karson's. She wants him to have it."

"That's quite the gift." Restoring a junkyard car would not have been cheap. "But if she's got money to burn."

"Londyn saved for a long time to restore that car," Gemma fired back. "It was important to her and she worked hard for it."

I shrugged. I didn't care. This was just conversation and a way to pass the time. I wasn't all that interested in Gemma's life story and how she'd come here. I was interested in when she'd be leaving.

"Why are you in Montana if you're headed to California?"

"For Katherine." She glared. "I wanted to see her and to apologize."

"You two looked fairly chummy last night, drinking all the expensive wine."

"Is that what this is about? The profit margin? I'll pay for the wine, okay?"

Of course, she would. She was loaded. "We don't need your money."

"God, you're something else. First, I need to pay my way. Then, you're too good for my money. You haven't changed at all, have you? In eleven years, you still only know how to send one type of message: mixed."

"Mixed? I think my intentions the last time you were here were pretty fucking clear."

I'd wanted her. I'd told her I'd wanted her. Lying in my arms, I'd told her I'd thought we had something real.

And she'd left anyway.

"I didn't . . ." She blew out a deep breath. "I'm sorry."

It was too late for an apology. I didn't trust her, not after she'd snuck out of my bed and disappeared without so much as a word. All because she'd wanted to strike it rich.

"Keep up," I barked, pulling down the brim of my hat a fraction of an inch. Then I urged Jigsaw faster.

Today wasn't Gemma's first time on a horse. She

didn't need to be coddled. She was doing just fine walking, so we'd trot for a bit and put an end to this conversation.

The asshole who'd been pissed at her for eleven years wanted her to falter. To get scared and beg to slow down. To dent her confidence as way of punishment.

But I wasn't a complete asshole and when she stayed right by my side, actually seeming to enjoy the faster clip, another surge of pride swelled.

Gemma wasn't scared of anything, least of all me or a gentle horse.

She relaxed into the saddle, finding her rhythm with Sprite's, and by the time we made it through the loop and back to the stables, Gemma looked damn good on that horse.

Too good.

Her hair swung as she rode. Her thighs flexed and her breasts bounced. There was a peach flush to her cheeks and an added sparkle in her eyes. She looked beautiful. Satisfied.

Hell. What if she'd actually enjoyed herself and wanted to do this every day? I was on the lesson schedule all week.

The cool edge to the fall weather had been burned off by the bright morning sun, and the horses were panting by the time we walked them into the arena. I hopped off Jigsaw first, then took Sprite's reins from Gemma to hold them while she dismounted.

She gripped the horn, shifted in the saddle, then

swung her right leg up and over. She swayed on the ground but found her balance. Her hands were shaking and there was a bead of sweat by her temple.

I really was a dickhead, pushing her so hard. She might have liked it, but I'd still gone too far.

Before I could apologize, Gemma took Sprite's reins from my hand and forced a too-wide smile. "That was fun. I forgot how much I liked it here. Maybe I'll take Katherine up on her offer to stay a while."

My eyes narrowed, the apology forgotten. "What offer?"

"To stay in the guest bedroom at Cash and Katherine's place. I'm in no hurry to get to California. So maybe I'll stay."

I scoffed. "You'll make it a week, maybe two before you get bored."

"You're so sure you know me. That you have me pegged." Her eyes blazed defiance. "But you don't know shit."

"Oh, I know you. Intimately." I inched closer, the smell of her perfume hitting my nose. She held my gaze by raising her chin higher. Those luscious lips right there, positioned and ready for the taking.

If I kissed her, would she kiss me back? Or would I see the Cadillac's taillights racing toward the highway by supper?

"What do you want from me, Easton?"

For you to get the hell out of my head. "I want you to leave. You don't fit here."

I'd expected a snarky comeback. More of that stubborn, infuriating attitude that clearly hadn't changed in the years she'd been away. But something flashed in her eyes that looked a lot like sorrow.

She dropped her chin and unlocked her gaze, turning to stare off into the distance. "Maybe you're right. I'm not sure where I fit."

Her words were no more than a whisper, but they sent me rocking on my heels.

Gemma brushed past me, leading Sprite to the stables.

Son of a bitch. This wasn't my problem. If this road trip was Gemma's way to find herself, more power to her. *She. Is. Not. My. Problem.* So why wouldn't my heart climb down from my throat?

I gripped Jigsaw's reins and he followed me without hesitation into his stall.

Gemma was standing in Sprite's stall, pointing to the saddle. "What should I do?"

"I'll take care of it."

"Okay." She patted Sprite's cheek. "You did good. It was nice to meet you."

I took a step back, giving Gemma a wide berth to exit the stall. She gave me a small nod, then turned and walked down the center aisle. Lesson complete.

She wasn't the same girl who'd left here. I was man enough to admit she'd changed—not to her face, not today.

Gemma had grown into a mature, breathtaking woman. Even with the sadness in her eyes, the longing, she was close to irresistible.

But if I let myself worry about Gemma, I'd turn myself in knots.

"She's a good girl."

"Shit." I jumped at Grandma's voice, slapping a hand over my heart. "Give a guy a warning."

She laughed, watching as Gemma disappeared around the corner and into the sunshine. "How was the lesson?"

"Fine."

"She's lost, that girl. Always has been. She's running from anything that makes her feel."

I frowned. "She screwed Kat over. You remember how upset Kat was when Gemma ditched her."

"She was nineteen years old, Easton. I recall a few mistakes you made at that age. There was the time you stole your dad's car and drove into town to get drunk at the bar. There was the time you—"

"All right, all right." I held up a hand. "You've made your point."

"Katherine has chosen to forgive her and welcome her here. We can all do the same. For however long she wants to stay."

I swallowed a groan. "She'll leave."

"I'm not so sure. Not this time."

I wouldn't argue with Grandma, but her soft spot for Gemma had made her blind. There was nothing for

Gemma to do here. She wasn't cut out for ranch work. She'd be bored working for Kat in one of the trivial jobs at the lodge. And where was she going to live? Cash and Kat's guest bedroom?

She'd stay and this vacation of hers would run its course, then she'd be gone.

I just had to wait it out. Stay away from Gemma so that the second time around, I didn't fall into her trap.

And make the same mistake twice.

CHAPTER SIX

GEMMA

"Knock. Knock." I inched Katherine's office door open and peeked inside.

"Hey." She waved me in. "What's up?"

"I need to ask you a question and I need the answer to be yes."

"Okay," she drawled. "Should I be nervous?"

"Probably." I plopped down in a chair across from her desk.

Katherine's hair was pulled into a ponytail and she was wearing a long-sleeved zip-up with the resort's name embroidered on the chest. She looked comfortable yet authoritative.

I had the comfort with my jeans and black sweater, but I lacked authority.

I *missed* authority.

"I'm bored," I admitted. "Like, going-out-of-my-mind bored. Can I have a job? Please?"

It had been three days since I'd gone on my ride with Easton, and I'd spent those days largely in my room. It was easier to avoid him while locked inside. I'd passed the days by reading and pestering Benjamin. After my seventh call in seventy-two hours, he'd threatened to block my number. There were zero emails in my inbox and I'd poured over my financial statements with more attention to detail than I had in the past five years—total.

My life had gone from ninety miles per hour to a standstill gridlock. This morning, I'd admitted defeat.

Vacation pace was highly overrated and simply not for me.

I needed to work.

Katherine blinked. "A job?"

"Dusting. Cooking. Scrubbing toilets. I'll do anything. But I don't want to leave yet and if I spend another day in my room reading, I might die."

"But you're on vacation."

I grimaced. "I hate that word."

"Why not do the four-wheeler excursion? Or hike? Or go for another ride?"

"Thanks, but no, thanks," I muttered.

It was too risky outside. It was much safer indoors where Easton avoided me and I had more places to hide.

"You don't have to pay me," I said. "Just give me something to do so I don't sit around and dwell on the fact that last month, my life had purpose. And now the only thing I have in my future is a long trip to California in someone else's car. Please. Pleasepleaseplease. Give me toilet bowl duty."

Katherine giggled. "You're sure?"

"Positive."

She picked up the headset to her desk phone and dialed a number. "Hey, Annabeth, it's Kat."

Kat. I was still getting used to her nickname. To me, she'd always be Katherine.

"I have someone here who'll be working temporarily for the resort. Would you mind if I send her your way?" She paused, the smile growing on her face. "Great. Thanks. She'll be right over."

"Thank you," I said as she put the headset into its cradle.

"You're welcome. Annabeth is in charge of the staffers. She coordinates the housekeeping, food service and front desk crews." She pointed to a wall of bookshelves. "Her office is two doors down. She'll get you through the HR paperwork and find something for you."

"I mean it. Don't pay me." It wasn't like I needed the money, something Katherine had learned over a dinner. The two of us had spent every night in the dining room, eating decadent meals and consuming an exorbitant amount of wine.

This week, we'd pulled on our old friendship and I hadn't been surprised when it had fit like my favorite sweater. I'd forgotten how easy it was to talk to Katherine. How comfortable and effortlessly the conversation flowed. We'd talked about everything, from her time with the Greers to my experiences in Boston.

The only time I'd dodged a topic had been when Easton's name was dropped.

That man . . . grr. I wanted to strangle him and kiss him and kick him and lick him all in the same moment.

Katherine had asked me how the ride had gone and I'd lied through my teeth. It hadn't been horrible. Riding Sprite had actually been fun, but with Easton there, infuriating me with every word muttered from that delicious mouth, it had been nearly impossible to enjoy myself.

Easton was loyal and proud. He was punishing me for screwing up years ago, with him and with Katherine. It would be a lot easier to dislike him if he didn't have grounds for his attitude.

It would be a lot easier to hate him if he wasn't so damn attractive.

The way that man looked on the horse, his eyes hooded by the brim of his hat, was grossly unfair. No one in Boston would believe that Gemma Lane, always composed and sophisticated, would be lusting after a rugged cowboy with dirt on his jeans and a smudge on his cheek.

Until they saw him, then no one would fault me.

"Dinner tonight?" I asked Katherine. If she said no, I'd probably drive into town and get a little space from the ranch. It was much too easy to think of Easton when I was here. Especially in my room, sitting on the bed. Or when I was in the shower. Or when I was breathing.

"Yes, but I was hoping you'd be up for a change of scenery. Friday nights we always eat dinner at Jake and Carol's. It's a family tradition."

"Oh, then that's okay." I wasn't part of the family and there was one family member in particular I was hoping to avoid until Montana was a smudge in the Cadillac's rearview mirror. "You go. I was thinking about driving into town anyway to see what's changed."

The Greer Ranch was located ten miles outside the small town of Clear River. From what I remembered, there wasn't much more than a gas station, post office, café and a bar in town, but it was better than nothing.

"Not happening, sweetheart." My head whipped around to the voice behind me as Carol marched into Katherine's office. Her white hair hung loose today, draped over her shoulders. "You're coming to dinner."

"But—"

She held up a hand. "Think of it as a peace offering."

"A peace offering? For what?"

"For the little arrangement you two girls made behind my back." Carol aimed her finger at Katherine. "Don't think I didn't notice Gemma's credit card on her room."

"Oh. That," I muttered.

"I told you that you weren't paying, but if it means that much to you, then I'll let it slide. But you're coming to dinner. We eat at six o'clock. Be early. You two can ride together since you haven't been to our new place."

"Sounds good." Katherine didn't bother arguing. It would be pointless.

"I'm going to go." I stood from the chair, gave Katherine a wide-eyed look, then scurried from her office before Carol could rope me into any other family functions.

Two doors down, I knocked on the half-open door and met my new boss, Annabeth, who I liked immediately. She was in her mid-fifties with warm eyes and a cute blond bob. We chatted briefly about my work history and situation here—the way I was leveraging my friendship with Katherine to score a job to keep me occupied—and she promised to be gentle with me since I hadn't had a boss in over seven years.

Annabeth hired me as an unpaid intern. I'd never been an intern before or unpaid, but when she took me to the front desk and explained my new duties, I'd accepted them with a genuine smile.

The resort hadn't had a receptionist in three weeks, not since the previous one had moved to Texas. It was the reason Carol had greeted me when I'd arrived earlier this week. So here I was, ready to greet anyone who walked through the front door.

There wasn't much walk-in traffic at a five-star mountain resort that filled its rooms with long-term, advance reservations. But when guests did come through the lobby, it was nice to have someone there to greet them—besides Clive the elk.

After signing a handful of employment papers and a brief tutorial on the computer system, Annabeth left me on my own, promising I'd be bored in minutes.

She wasn't wrong.

But being bored at the front desk was better than being bored in my room.

I spent a couple hours getting familiar with the computer system, poking around the events calendar and reservation software, both of which were relatively intuitive. Carol brought me a ham sandwich from the kitchen at noon—my agreed-upon salary with Annabeth—and ate with me at the desk.

We talked about Jake and the ranch and how she wished Cash would *open his damn eyes.*

She didn't elaborate on that one. Not that she needed to.

After lunch, she went back to work doing whatever it was Carol did and I manned my station at the desk. Few guests entered the lobby and when they did, I waved and inquired about their day. I played solitaire, partaking in the occasional staring contest with Clive—he won two out of three—until the clock neared five, my shift was over, and it was time to head to my room to freshen up before dinner.

I'd just closed down the computer when footsteps sounded beyond the door, lifting my spirits at the anticipation of another rare guest interaction. I squared my shoulders and readied my smile, but when the door opened, my expression dropped. "Oh, it's you."

Easton narrowed his eyes as he walked into the lobby. "What are you doing?"

"Working."

His jaw ticked. "What?"

"I'm working. Katherine hired me this morning."

"Like hell she did."

I rolled my eyes. "I'm here, Easton. Deal with it."

He gave me his famous silent, brooding stare.

"I'm not leaving." Yet.

"Because you have nowhere else to go, so you'll just leach off us here until you're ready."

"I'm not leaching." *What a jerk.* "But no, I don't have anywhere else to go at the moment, so it looks like you're stuck with me."

He arched an eyebrow and headed straight for the stairs. Conversation over. I'd been dismissed.

I didn't let myself watch him walk away.

Grr. No one had ever climbed under my skin as quickly as Easton. One of these days, I was going to do something to shock that hard, unwavering scowl off his handsome face.

I'd once been so desperate for eye contact from that man. I'd been the nineteen-year-old girl trying not to be affected when he walked into the room. The one trying not to look at him because it stung deep when he'd never looked back. Easton had always had better things to do than bother with me.

Not much had changed.

Except me.

I no longer had anything to prove. I'd shown the world I was more than where I'd come from. I'd made my mark, my fortune and fame.

And I'd learned the hard way it was just as hollow as the home where I'd been born.

This journey was about searching for a real life. The life money couldn't buy.

I wanted the things I'd never had.

Family. Love. Peace.

Chasing down riches was easy. I could do that—I *had* done that.

There was no easy way to find the safety and security that came with love and family. People were either born with it, or they weren't. For those of us who weren't, letting others in meant exposing your weaknesses. It meant trusting others not to break your heart.

The concept was easy enough to grasp. Dr. Brewer and I had talked for years about my talent for maintaining emotional distance from others, even my friends. The problem *was* me. The solution was me too.

But letting someone share your life . . . they could turn it all upside down.

Because trust was something often betrayed, and innocence could be taken when the person you trusted didn't protect you.

Like a mother.

A mother who allowed a man to drag her fifteen-year-old daughter out of her bedroom simply because the guy wanted an audience while he got a blow job.

The chains wrapped around my heart were courtesy of her betrayals.

I blinked the memory away, refusing to think of my mother's face. It greeted me in the mirror each morning, and that was bad enough without letting myself revisit the past.

Hurrying upstairs to my room, I refreshed my makeup and brushed my hair. I touched up my lip gloss—three times—and changed my clothes twice. It was the fact that Easton would be at dinner that had me pacing my room, waiting for Katherine's knock. It came at precisely fifteen minutes to six.

"Ready?" she asked.

"Sure," I lied. I'd tamed cutthroat attorneys and ruthless fashion designers, so why was I so nervous about a family dinner?

"Easton just stopped by," she said as we walked down the hallway. "He told me to fire you."

"Stubborn ass," I muttered.

"Don't worry. I told him to mind his own side of the business."

I frowned and followed her downstairs, making our

way through the rear exit where she'd parked her truck. "So who's going to be at dinner?"

"The usual suspects. Carol and Jake. JR and Liddy."

I nodded, remembering Easton's parents. "I always liked Liddy."

"She's a sweetheart. And then the guys. Just family tonight. That's the rule."

The Greers and Katherine. *Just family.* I was happy that she'd found one. But where did that put me? "Should I be going? I feel like I'm intruding."

"You're not. And besides, it's too late now." She laughed as she drove. "If you don't show up with me, Carol will just come and collect you herself."

We bounced along the gravel road, driving toward the mountains that had greeted me each morning this week. When a house came into view beside a grove of aspen trees, my mouth fell open. "Wow."

"Pretty, right? Carol wanted to coordinate the house with the lodge, so they went with the same look."

The dark wooden siding along with the stonework out front was rustic yet classy. The house was warm and inviting but too big to be considered cozy. It was the castle for a Montana working couple who'd earned their retirement.

A line of dirty vehicles crowded the long gravel drive-way, and before we were even parked, the front door opened. Carol's white hair caught the fading sunset's light, tinting the soft strands pink.

"I only have five bottles of wine," she said, waving us inside. "Save two for the rest of us, will you?"

Katherine and I both laughed as we stepped across the threshold. Then we were mobbed.

"Welcome back." Jake hugged me first, then pulled Katherine into his side, pinning her there.

Next came JR who clapped me on the back. "I'm Jake Junior. Or JR. Not sure if you remember me or not."

I smiled. "Of course, I do."

"Heard you're our newest employee."

"That's right," I said. Easton was standing in the living room, close enough to overhear. I shot him a smug grin. "Today was the first day of many."

He scowled and took a long drink from the beer bottle in his grip.

"Hi, Gemma." Liddy took her husband's place for a hug. "It's so nice seeing you again. Welcome back."

"Thank you for having me."

"Hey, again." Cash extended a hand from where he stood beside his mother.

"Hi, Cash." I shook his hand, taking in the similarities of the Greer men now that they were in the same room.

Easton inherited his father's and grandfather's black-coffee eyes, while Cash had gotten Liddy's hazel irises. But that seemed to be the only thing she'd passed to her sons. Otherwise, with their strong jaws and dark hair, Easton and Cash were younger versions of Jake and JR.

"Come on in and sit." Carol escorted us all to the long dining room off the kitchen.

Above the table, a bright glass chandelier illuminated the room. The table was a deep stained walnut, the top satiny smooth and each place set with a glossy cream plate.

"Liddy. JR. Cash. Katherine." Carol pointed to the assigned chairs as she fired names.

I held back a smile that she'd paired Cash and Katherine together. Then my heart dropped. Because there were two seats left beside each other.

One for me.

One for Easton.

Damn it, Carol.

"Wine?" JR offered, lifting a bottle after we'd taken our seats.

"Please." I held out my glass. *And keep it coming.*

Easton ripped his chair out, sitting down with a loud huff. The clank of his beer bottle hitting the table sent the message loud and clear. He was pissed I was here, and he was pissed he had to sit beside me.

I gave him a saccharine smile and held out my glass. "Cheers."

His lip curled.

"Cheers." Cash chuckled and came to my rescue, extending his beer bottle across the table to clink with mine. Then he tipped his bottle to Katherine's glass before taking a long pull.

I took a sip of mine as Liddy, seated to my left, held out her hand. She smiled sweetly.

What was she . . . *oh. Right.* The prayer. The entire table joined hands as Jake Sr. bowed from his seat at the head of the table.

I took Liddy's hand, then kept my eyes glued to my plate as I lifted my right into the air. It was up to Easton if he was going to touch me or not.

His hesitation was obvious.

The entire table waited. And waited.

Jake cleared his throat, and finally, Easton grabbed my hand, jerking my arm in the process as he lowered his chin.

The smell of his soap wafted to my nose. His face was clean shaven, and he must have showered between the time he'd seen me in the lobby and the time he'd come here because his hair was damp at the ends.

Easton's grip was rough, his callouses pressing into the tender skin of my palm as Jake prayed. Tingles shot up my arm and that scent of his was dizzying. But I'd held up under more extreme situations than this. I would not let myself drool.

"Amen."

The second the word echoed around the table, my hand was dropped like a hot coal.

Liddy gave my other hand a light squeeze, then let me go to drape a napkin in her lap.

I reached for my wine, sharing a look with Katherine across the table.

She lifted her glass in a sign of solidarity.

"So, Gemma." Jake scooped a heap of mashed potatoes onto his plate as the rest of the food began the circle around the table. "Katherine told me you drove here from Boston. That's quite a trip."

"Technically, I drove from West Virginia, but yes, it was a long trip. I have to say, the best part was through Montana. I'd forgotten how beautiful it was here."

"We sure are having a nice fall," Liddy said, passing me a bowl of green beans. "How long are you planning to stay?"

"Not long," Easton answered, before he drained the last swallow of his beer.

I shoved the bowl in his face. "Beans?"

He wrenched the dish from my grasp, grumbling something under his breath that earned him a scowl from Carol on his other side.

"How'd Rory do on the trail ride today?" JR asked Cash after the food had been passed around.

"Good. He's a quick learner and the guests like him."

"Maybe you should put him on the schedule," JR told Easton.

Beside me, his teeth ground together audibly. "I know how to delegate my staff. It was my idea to send him along with Cash in the first place."

The tension in the room grew thick. The plates and

the food were of sudden interest as all eyes dropped except for Easton's and JR's.

My plate was overloaded with mashed potatoes, roast beef, gravy, beans and a roll. It seemed like the perfect time to shove a huge bite into my mouth and occupy myself with chewing.

Was something happening on the ranch? Were Easton and JR fighting? If I wasn't sitting here, how would this conversation really have gone?

"Jake, I was hoping you could help me for a couple of weeks." Katherine was brave enough to break the silence. "I've got a project and need your expertise."

"I can probably do that." He nodded, aiming his eyes to Easton. "That means you'll need to handle the equipment and prepping the snowmobiles for winter."

"I know." He sighed. "I've got it covered."

Why was I suddenly feeling bad for the guy who'd been a jackass to me this week? His shoulders were bunched and his back stiff. The frustration radiating off Easton's body was palpable.

Part of me wanted to put my hand on his forearm and give him a reassuring smile. The other part remembered . . . jackass. Besides, whatever this family dynamic was, it was not my business.

"Gemma, we never did hear *your* answer to Mom's question." Cash sent his brother a smirk. "How long are you staying?"

"I'm not sure exactly. Maybe for a few weeks.

Katherine said something about an empty guest bedroom at your place."

Easton scoffed.

I ignored him.

But Carol wasn't having it. "What is your problem tonight?"

"She's not staying, Grandma."

"That's not really up to you, is it?" she snapped.

Easton put down his fork. "I'm not saying she *can't* stay. I'm just saying she won't."

Really? Because to me, it sounded a lot like him telling me I couldn't stay.

"And why not?" Katherine asked.

"She's like the guests here, Kat. They love Montana for a week. But soon, she'll be ready to get back to the city. Back to her manicures and massages and Starbucks. This isn't the place for her."

"And who the hell are you to dictate the place for me?" I twisted in my chair, meeting his glare with one of my own.

"I'm calling it like I see it."

"Well, you're wrong."

"Yeah? You won't last a month. Hell, you only made it a few days before you went running to Kat because you were bored."

I guess Katherine had told him the reason for my sudden employment. When I glanced her way, she mouthed, "Sorry."

"I like to be busy."

"Sure," he deadpanned.

I leaned in closer, sitting taller in my chair. "You truly are an asshole."

The table snickered around us but I kept my eyes locked on Easton's.

He leaned closer, his breath caressing my cheek as he taunted, "But am I wrong?"

"Yes."

"Prove it."

"By staying? No problem. That was already my plan."

"Like I said. You won't make it a month."

"I bet she makes it past Christmas." JR chuckled. "Just to prove you wrong, son."

Easton gave his dad a scowl, then turned to the meal, shoveling a bite of potatoes in his mouth.

"I think it will be wonderful to have you here through the holidays," Liddy said.

Wait. What? When had I agreed to stay for Christmas? That was over three months away.

"I appreciate the offer, but I don't think Katherine and Cash want me living with them for three months. I'd love to stay for a few weeks, but months? I, uh . . ."

A slow, evil grin spread across Easton's face as he chewed.

Bastard.

Katherine had offered me a guest room, but for three months? That wasn't a guest. That was a roommate.

"Gemma will stay at the cabin," Carol announced.

"Huh?" I was getting whiplash. "What cabin?"

"The one Jake and I built when we first moved here. It's a little old and outdated but it's all yours."

Fantastic. Easton had all but dared me to stay, and now there were no excuses to why I couldn't.

"The cabin it is." My cheery voice betrayed my terror.

Easton's smug grin dropped.

Good.

He'd baited me. He'd flustered me and now I was in Montana for three months because there was no way I was letting him win. Even if that meant crashing in an old cabin.

I'd show him.

Ugh.

What the hell had I just gotten myself into?

CHAPTER SEVEN

GEMMA

"Are you sure you want to do this?" Katherine asked.

I shrugged and looked around the room. The place had running water and electricity, luxuries I didn't take for granted. "It's not that bad. I mean, it's not my posh room at the lodge, but it's a thousand times nicer than our tent at the junkyard."

"True."

"This will be great," I promised. "It's a nice cabin."

"If you change your mind, you're always welcome to our guest room."

"Thanks." I'd been living alone for a long time and actually preferred having this older cabin to myself than sharing someone's space.

The last roommate I'd had was Katherine. We'd stayed together in the tent, then here when we'd been in the staff quarters.

Whenever the two of us had been bored, we'd practiced our poker skills. Karson had taught us in the junkyard. We never had money to bet, but we'd play and practice with toothpicks.

"Do you still remember how to play poker?" I asked, setting down my suitcase in the middle of the cabin's living room.

"Absolutely." Katherine walked over to the kitchen, running a finger through the dust on the countertop. "About a year after you left, Cash was home for spring break or something and he came over to the staff quarters. Some of the guys were having a poker tournament. I asked if I could play too. They all teased me that they didn't have time to teach a girl how to play."

"Did you win?"

"Hell, yes, I won." She laughed. "Every once in a while, Cash and I go into town to play at the bar. They have games on Friday and Saturday nights. You should come with us next time."

"Maybe." Though I hadn't played in years. "So what's the story with you and Cash?"

"No story." She shook her head. "We're roommates. Coworkers. Friends."

Lies. She was in love with him. And Cash was oblivious.

But I wasn't one to lecture on matters of men. I was staying in an old cabin that needed a deep clean because I'd let a man bait me into a foolish challenge two days ago.

Thankfully, Londyn didn't care how long it took me to get to California. I'd called her after the family dinner and told her everything. Once she'd finished laughing her ass off, she'd told me I had no choice but to show Easton up.

So here I was, in a Montana cabin for the next three months.

"It's a good thing we raided a cleaning cart." Katherine opened the refrigerator and cringed at the smell, shutting it quickly. "No one would think less of you if you said screw this and left."

"Easton would."

"Does his opinion really matter?"

Yes. "No, but I like it here. So why not shut him up?"

"If you're sure."

I nodded. "I'm sure."

The truth was, I'd contemplated leaving. After the dinner, I'd thought about getting in the Cadillac and abandoning this ridiculous notion. I'd considered it a lot in the past forty-eight hours. It was Sunday and if I left tomorrow morning, I'd be in sunny California before the end of the week.

But I wasn't ready to go.

Besides the benefit of proving Easton wrong, I was enjoying my time here. Katherine and I were bonding. The Greer family was incredibly welcoming and my simple job at the front desk was refreshing.

Every time I heard Easton's voice in the back of my

mind, telling me I didn't belong, I shut it up by finding something about this situation that appealed.

This cabin was one. It was two miles from the lodge, nestled in a clearing of evergreens. There wasn't a sprawling mountain view or an on-call masseuse. But it was my own space, peaceful and secluded. I had room to think. To start deciding what I would do with my life once these three months were over and my trip to California was complete.

Because at the moment, I didn't have a damn clue. I needed this time to reflect. To plan.

Besides, I could survive anything for three months.

And I'd lived in far, far worse places.

"What's your plan for today?" Katherine asked.

"Clean."

"Want some help?"

"Nah. I don't mind. You go and enjoy your day off."

"Day off?" She gave me a quizzical look. "What's that? I'm going to the office to catch up on emails. Maybe, if I'm lucky, I can squeeze in a ride this afternoon. Want to join me?"

"Maybe. Shoot me a text."

"Okay." She took another look around the open room and her eyes widened. "Good luck."

I laughed and walked her outside, leaning on one of the porch's log posts as she got into her truck parked beside the Cadillac. "Bye."

She waved. "Bye."

As her truck disappeared around the curve in the road, I took a long breath of the clean, mountain air, then made my way inside the cabin.

The smell was musty. Dust floated everywhere, catching the glint of sunlight attempting to stream through the filmy windows. Carol had offered to clean the cabin because no one had stayed here in over three years—she'd come out to tidy up and check for mice a few times each year but otherwise the place had been empty—but I'd declined her offer, insisting on doing the work myself.

In a way, cleaning would make it my own.

I whipped off my sweater, folding it and setting it on my suitcase, then I got to work.

The bulk of the cabin was one large room. The living area was no more than a rawhide couch, a matching chair and a coffee table. Opposite it was a two-seat table and a small kitchen. The rear half of the cabin had the single bedroom. It was cramped with a queen-sized bed and a set of dresser drawers. The adjoining bathroom was designed for function with only a standing shower crammed beside the sink and toilet. The square laundry room by the back door doubled as the pantry and storage room.

I tackled the bedroom first, wanting to get my things put away. There was a canvas tarp over the bed to keep it from getting dusty, but I still stripped the quilt and sheets and tossed them into the washing machine. Then I dusted every surface and wiped out the dresser's drawers before sweeping and mopping.

Sweat beaded on my brow after I was done with the kitchen, having washed all the dishes, then scrubbed the floor on my hands and knees.

Even with the lack of care, it didn't take me long to make my way through the cabin, because it was just that small.

I opened the door to let in the fresh air and did the same to the windows once they were clean. The smile on my face felt earned. Carefree. I'd worked my ass off since the day I'd run away from home at sixteen, first to simply stay alive, then to make something of myself. Accomplishment gave me satisfaction.

Or at least, it had. The past year in Boston had lacked fulfillment.

What I'd needed was a hard day of cleaning where I could see my work unfold before my eyes.

Three months here? Piece of cake.

I was one laundry room away from a sparkling cabin when I heard a truck approach. My mood tanked when I saw its driver.

"What is he doing here," I muttered from the cabin's porch.

Easton parked beside the Cadillac and hopped out, not sparing me a glance as he walked to the back and hefted out a huge cooler. "Where do you want this?"

"Uh, what is it?"

"Food. Mom didn't want you running to the store, so she spent yesterday in the kitchen."

Liddy had cooked.

For me.

My own mother hadn't cooked for me. But his had. My heart squeezed as he walked up the porch stairs carrying the cooler.

Easton scanned me from head to toe, and like always, he frowned.

I glanced down at my jeans and the gray tank top I'd had underneath my sweater. "What?"

"Nothing." He brushed past me and stomped inside.

"Take off your boots. I just cleaned." I bit the inside of my cheeks to keep from laughing as he spun around and gaped. "Kidding."

Easton didn't find me funny.

I followed him to the kitchen, leaving the front door open, as he set the cooler beside the fridge. He bent and flipped open the lid to start unloading, but I waved him away. "I'll take care of it."

"'Kay." He stood and walked outside.

"Goodbye," I called after him, then turned my attention to the cooler. "Nice to see you too. And thanks. I *did* do a great job cleaning. How kind of you to notice."

"Talking to yourself?"

I jumped at Easton's voice. "I thought you left."

He hefted a tote in the air. "Wine. From my grandma."

"Carol gets me." I stood and took the tote from him, setting it on the counter. Then I waited, assuming he'd actually leave this time unless there were more gifts in his truck.

But he didn't leave. Easton walked into the living room and ran a hand through that thick, soft hair as he glanced around. He'd traded his normal, long-sleeved plaid shirt for a fitted thermal. The textured cotton stretched across his biceps, showcasing the strength of his arms. It molded to his torso and that flat stomach.

If he'd just smile, a little, he'd be so incredibly handsome. Gruff and stoic worked for Easton. The man was a challenge and an enigma. His serious composure gave nothing away and that was a turn-on for a woman like me who enjoyed the uphill battle.

I'd learned in my week here that he didn't have a wife or girlfriend, but I had no doubt the local ladies swooned over his rugged, somber exterior. But a smile . . . damn, I wanted to see a smile.

I'd seen it once—eleven years ago when he'd taken me to his bed, and I hadn't forgotten it in all this time.

Easton's smile was unmatched. It was rare. Maybe the reason it was so special was because he gave it to so few people.

"Looks good in here."

My hand flew to my heart and I feigned surprise. "Was that . . . a compliment? Did you actually say something nice to me?"

His lips pursed into a thin line.

"Oh, relax." I turned to the cupboards and opened

the one where I'd found glasses earlier. "Would you like to stay for a glass of wine? Or has five minutes in my presence irritated you enough to leave me alone for a week?"

"I don't drink wine."

"Of course, you don't." It probably went against the cowboy code to drink anything but milk, water, black coffee, beer and whiskey neat.

"But I'll take a glass of water."

Seriously? I'd been joking in the invite. Why would he take it? What was he up to? I didn't ask as I filled his glass from the tap, but I kept an eye on him as I uncorked a bottle of Cabernet. I'd thank Carol later for including the opener in my tote bag.

"Here you go." I handed him his water as I joined him in the living room.

Easton took it and sat on the couch, tossing one long arm over the back. Then he lifted an ankle, crossing it over a knee.

"What do you want?" I sat in the chair and cut right to the chase. Easton wasn't here to be friendly.

"You. Gone."

"You'll get your wish in three months."

He studied me, his gaze full of scrutiny.

"What? No reminders that I won't make it?" I asked.

"No. You know how I feel."

"Yes, you've made it crystal clear. So I'd say we're at a stalemate."

"Guess so." He drained his water with three long gulps. The bob of his Adam's apple was mesmerizing.

I expected him to leave with the glass empty, but once again, he stayed seated, settling deeper into the couch. "Don't you have somewhere to be?"

"No." He looked around the room, his eyes taking it all in. "When Cash and I were little, Dad would take us camping here. Boys only. We'd go fishing at the creek. He'd build a fire and we'd have a cookout outside. I haven't been inside in ages. Every time I come back, it seems smaller."

Why was he telling me this? Again, I didn't verbalize my question. Because when Easton wasn't snapping at me or barking something condescending, I soaked up his every word. Especially if it had a thing to do with his youth.

Because his childhood was my dream.

"Do you know how to use that?" He pointed a finger at the wood stove in the corner.

"Uh . . ." I glanced around, searching the walls for a thermostat. There wasn't one. "No. I don't."

"I'll show you."

"I can figure it out."

"And burn down a Greer family legacy? I'm not taking that chance." He stood and walked to the stove. "Come here."

"Ask me nicely."

He shot a look over his shoulder that wasn't exactly a glare, but it wasn't polite.

I enjoyed a warm house too much to annoy him, so I set my wine on the coffee table and joined him in a crouch by the stove. There was a small stack of wood and a basketful of newspaper beside it, along with a long-handled lighter.

Easton showed me how to use the paper and kindling to get it going, then gave me instruction on how to set the airflow. Within minutes, the fire was roaring, chasing away any of the chill in the air.

"Thanks." I stood and went to close the windows.

I left the door open, assuming he'd leave at any minute. Then I went to unpack the cooler, stacked full of plastic containers. "She made all this in a day? It's more food than I'll eat alone in a month."

Easton crossed the room, closing the front door, and joined me at the fridge. "Want some help?"

"Unpacking? No, I've got it."

"No, not unpacking. Eating."

I blinked up at him as he leaned a shoulder against the fridge. "You want to stay for dinner?"

"Mom made my favorite ham and potato casserole. She only makes it for special occasions and because you're our guest, you got it."

Ah. So that was why he was here. "Jealous?"

"If you're not going to eat all this food, I'll take that casserole off your hands."

"Too bad. It's mine." And I was going to eat it first.

Any meal that made Easton act remotely civil must be outstanding.

He shoved off the fridge. "Come on. Give it to me so someone who will actually appreciate it will eat it."

"Excuse me?" I surged to my feet. "I don't think you get to tell me what I appreciate. For a guy who has never gone hungry a day in his life, I can assure you, I appreciate each and every meal I eat."

Easton winced and the annoyed look on his face vanished. "Sorry."

I crossed my arms over my chest.

"That casserole is important." He sighed. "To my family."

"A casserole."

"Yes. It was my grandmother's recipe. My mom's mom. She died before I was born in a house fire. Not much survived the blaze except some of her jewelry that was in a fire-safe box and a few recipe cards she kept in a metal tin. That casserole was Mom's favorite too. The reason she only makes it for special occasions is because it's hard for her to see my grandma's handwriting."

My anger vanished. "And she made it for me."

"She made it for you. So if you're not going to eat it and fuss over it and make sure Mom knows exactly how much you appreciate the heartache it took for her to make you that meal, then give it to me so I can."

"Okay."

"Okay." He went to grab it from the cooler, but I slapped his hand away.

"I'm not giving it to you. But you can stay for dinner. And we can both make sure she knows how much it was appreciated."

Not his first choice, but he kept his mouth shut and nodded.

Most of the time, I wanted to strangle Easton. But then there were moments like this one where he showed me a glimpse of the good man lurking inside that solid body. The man who would come here and suffer through a meal with a woman he couldn't stand, just so the next day he could make sure his mother felt appreciated and that her grief had not gone unnoticed.

I glanced at the clock on the microwave and saw it was nearly five. "Are you hungry now?"

He shrugged. "I could eat."

"Then I'll get it started." I went about preparing our meal, following the instruction card Liddy had taped to the casserole's aluminum dish. While it was in the oven, I set the small table while Easton went outside to bring in some more chopped wood to set beside the stove.

"Is that always here?" I asked as he stacked the split logs. "The firewood."

"No, I, uh . . . I brought it over yesterday."

"You?" My jaw dropped.

"As tempting as it is to let the snow and cold chase you away, the last thing we need is a city girl freezing to death on ranch property. Goes against the sales brochure for the resort."

I snorted. "Was that a joke? Who knew Easton Greer has a sense of humor buried beneath the snide remarks and muttered censure?"

He frowned.

Predictable, this man. "Ah, there's the face I recognize. I was worried for a moment."

The timer dinged on the oven before he could deliver a snarky comeback. I smiled to myself as I took dinner from the oven. Tonight's banter felt different than our normal bickering. It was almost fun. Charged.

It felt a lot like foreplay.

Not that Easton had any notions of taking me to bed. At least, not again.

With our plates served, we sat and began the meal in silence, neither one of us doing more than shovel those first few bites.

"Wow. This is amazing." The casserole was the definition of comfort food. It was warm and cheesy with just the right amount of salt and those blessed starchy potatoes.

"Told you," he said, dishing his plate with seconds. "You and Kat seem to be getting along."

"We always did. Before I left."

"You lived together, right? In California?"

I wasn't sure where this curiosity was coming from, but I'd take conversation over a quiet meal. I'd eaten alone enough times in my life to prefer company, even if it was grouchy. "In a junkyard outside of Temecula."

"When Kat told us about that, I didn't believe her at first. Not because I thought she was dishonest. It just didn't seem . . . I couldn't wrap my head around it."

"That's because you grew up with a family in a loving home." I'd told my story to enough people to know the reason Easton struggled to understand—he had good parents.

"There were six of you?"

"Yes. One of the kids lived in the neighborhood where I grew up. Karson. He ran away when he was sixteen, and since it seemed like a damn good idea, I left too." After a particularly bad night at home, I'd finally had enough. "It was impulsive," I told Easton. "I didn't have a bag packed. There was no preparation. No stack of cash hidden underneath my mattress or a stash of extra clothes and food. One day I lived with my mother. The next day, I lived with Karson in a junkyard and slept on the dirt."

"Jesus." His fork was frozen midair. His eyes were filled with pity.

"Don't do that," I whispered. "Don't pity me. Just believe me when I tell you that the junkyard was the better place. Running away was the best decision I've ever made."

If Easton asked for more details, I wasn't sure I had the strength to talk about it tonight. I didn't talk about that time with anyone but Dr. Brewer, and even then, I'd stopped seeing her four years ago.

Some memories were better left in the murky corners of our minds where, if we were lucky, they'd eventually fade.

"Londyn came along after me." I forced a smile as I ate another bite. "Her parents were drug addicts."

"Katherine's were too, right?"

I nodded. "Her mom. I don't think she ever knew her dad. Karson was working at a car wash and met her. She was begging for change, so he brought her to the junkyard that day. Introduced us. She actually went home after that, then showed up two weeks later with a garbage bag full of clothes and a black eye."

Easton's hand gripped his fork so hard I worried the metal would snap. "She didn't tell us that."

"We don't like to talk about it."

"That's fucked up," he said. "Not that you don't like to talk about it. The black eye."

You have no idea. "After Katherine came two other girls. Twins. Aria and Clara lived in Londyn's trailer park with their uncle after their parents died in a car crash. The uncle was mentally off. Creeped the hell out of me the one and only time I saw him." The image of his beady eyes still gave me the shivers. "They came to the junkyard one day, holding hands and wearing backpacks, and that made six."

"You were just kids. Living in the dirt." He shook his head, his lashes lifting. When his eyes met mine, they weren't full of pity this time. They were soft. Kind. He almost looked . . . proud. "And you just sold your company for twelve million dollars. Good for you, Gemma. Good for you."

Whether it was his expression or the sincerity of his words, I wasn't sure. But I wanted so badly in that moment to cry. To let Easton be nice to me and stop holding up that arm that kept everyone at a distance.

But I didn't cry.

I didn't lower my arm.

Instead I lifted my glass and gulped the last swallow of my wine.

Then I picked a fight.

"Do you like your job as assistant manager of the ranch?"

CHAPTER EIGHT

EASTON

Assistant manager.

That woman knew exactly where my hot buttons were and just how hard to poke them.

It had been two weeks since I'd stormed out of the cabin, irritated and angry that she'd known damn well I was in charge of the ranch but had purposefully pissed me off.

If Gemma wasn't running from people, she was shoving them away.

For the past two weeks, we'd stayed clear of one another. At least, as well as we could considering we worked together and my family had pulled Gemma into the fold.

My family loved her, especially Grandma and Mom.

After Mom's casserole, Gemma had sent her a bouquet of two dozen roses, delivered all the way from

Missoula, as a thank-you for the meals. Grandma had received a case of expensive wine the next day.

Whenever I'd come to the lodge, she'd be at the front desk with a smile waiting. Though never for me. Those smiles would vanish the second I walked through the door. But it was nice to have a cheerful face behind that desk.

For the guests.

The only reason I wasn't using the rear entrance was because the parking lot behind the lodge was always crowded with staff rigs. My trips to the lodge had nothing to do with Gemma or her smile.

And this trip to the cabin was out of necessity, not because I hadn't seen her in three days.

My truck bounced on the rough road. There seemed to be more bumps than normal. I made a mental note to have Granddad find Gemma an old truck to drive around since this wouldn't be good for the Cadillac.

If that car got ruined, well, it would be a travesty to the American classic.

And Gemma was staying.

My plan had backfired—something I wouldn't admit no matter how many times Cash had razzed me about it this week.

If she was staying, we'd have to make sure she had the right tools to survive on the ranch and in the cabin through the winter.

The leaves on the trees had mostly fallen over the past two weeks, the orange and yellow littering the ground and fading to brown. This fall had been short thanks to the cold patch that had swooped in over the past week. Every night had dropped below freezing and we weren't even ten days into October.

Next week's forecast was calling for snow.

I was simply glad we'd moved the cattle out of the mountains, even if Dad had gotten his way and they'd been put in the exact opposite pastures where I'd planned to have them.

We'd argued. He'd won.

Yesterday, I'd been so frustrated I'd spent my day working alone.

A plume of smoke rose above the patch of pine trees, and as I rounded the last corner of the road, the cabin came into view and I saw Gemma outside, her arms loaded with wood. The sound of my diesel caught her ears and she stopped, watching me pull into the space beside her Cadillac.

"Hey," I said as I hopped out.

"Hi." She gave me a small smile and disappeared inside. When she came back out to the porch, she brushed at the flecks of bark that had stuck to her sweater.

This one was olive, the same as the first day she'd arrived nearly a month ago. She looked pretty and relaxed, standing there in the doorway to the cabin. Her hair was up in a ponytail that flowed over her shoulder in loose waves.

Breathe, East. She's just a beautiful woman.

"What's up?" she asked.

I cleared my throat and jerked my chin to the bed of the truck. "I've got a load of wood for you."

"Thanks. I was starting to run low." She rubbed her hands up and down her arms, shivering at a gust of wind. "It's been cold."

"This should last you a couple of weeks."

"Let me grab my coat and I'll help."

"All right." Maybe the chivalrous thing to do would be unload the half cord myself. But I'd grown up with grandparents who'd worked side by side their entire lives. My parents too. And Gemma wasn't the type who'd sit by and idly watch someone else work.

I dug another pair of leather gloves from the jockey box of my truck and laid them on the tailgate for her. Then I started hauling loads to the metal rack Granddad had welded together fifty-some years ago.

Gemma joined right in, not saying much as we crossed paths. Every time I walked to the truck, she walked away from it with wood in her arms. Then I'd load up and we'd do the reverse.

It meant with every trip, we'd share an awkward glance, so I pushed harder, trying to change the timing. But the faster I pushed, she pushed. No matter how quickly I walked or loaded, she was keeping pace.

No one could accuse Gemma of slacking.

When the split logs we could reach from the ground were stacked, I nodded for Gemma to climb in. "Why don't you hop in the back and push the wood toward the tailgate."

"Okay." One of those long legs lifted and in a swift motion she was up.

That should not have been a sexy move but my dick jerked. Her legs, encased in faded jeans, were at eye level. When she bent, I had the perfect view of her ass and my palms twitched, wanting to squeeze her curves and mold them to mine. *Fuck.* This was the reason I'd been avoiding her for two weeks. Because every night when I went home, I had to jack off in the shower to the image of her legs wrapped around my hips and my greedy hands on her body.

Gemma and I argued. We were at each other's throats, and it was because if we didn't fight this attraction, if we gave in . . . we'd be doomed.

I dropped my gaze and focused on the job at hand, refusing to look at her until the work was done.

When the last log was stacked, she hopped down and I slammed the tailgate closed.

"Thanks." She removed the gloves I'd lent her and handed them over.

"No problem."

"How long did it take to cut and split all that?"

I shrugged. "A few hours."

This was what I'd done yesterday when I'd escaped to work alone.

"I appreciate it," she said.

"I know." Gemma, unlike a lot of people with her substantial wealth, appreciated effort from others. I waved and walked to my truck door, opening it up and was about to get in when she stopped me.

"Easton?"

"Yeah?"

"Want to stay for dinner?"

If I stayed, we'd probably get in a fight. It would be smarter to decline—I had work to do, and I'd already planned to stop by the lodge and grab dinner. Instead, I tossed the gloves into the truck and slammed the door. "Yeah."

It wasn't about the food.

It was Gemma.

She dropped her chin, hiding her smile as she walked past me and into the cabin.

I followed, toeing off my boots beside her shoes inside the door, then went to the fireplace to add another log. "Is it staying warm enough in here at night?"

"It's been great. Very cozy." She went to the fridge. "Beer, water or chocolate milk?"

Chocolate milk was a staple in my diet but I saw she had a glass of wine poured. "Beer, please."

She took out an amber bottle and twisted off the top, bringing it over for me in the living room. Then she returned to the kitchen where she'd been in the middle of chopping when I'd arrived. "We're having spaghetti."

"Want some help?"

"No, I'm good. This is easy."

I took a seat on the couch and looked around the room. It was the same cabin I'd known my whole life, the same furniture, but there was something different about it. It was cozier and more . . . intimate. Maybe that was because the wind was blowing outside, rustling the trees, and in here, there was the crackle of a fire, the scent of garlic and onions, and a beautiful woman standing in the kitchen, sipping wine and making us a meal.

It was impossible not to watch her as she moved. To appreciate the sway of her hips and the way her ponytail swished across the middle of her back. A lock of hair kept falling from where she'd tucked it behind her ear, and anytime she'd glance my way, there was a rosy flush to her cheeks.

She was bewitching. She pulled me into an alternate universe where there was just us.

"So you went from here to Boston, right?" I asked, needing to make some conversation before I did something hasty like get off this couch to kiss her in the kitchen. I didn't need to taste Gemma's lips. I had once and they'd been sweet and destructive, like a poisoned apple. So I'd keep my ass on this couch until it was time to leave.

"That's right." She nodded. "I assume you've been here since I left."

"Besides the occasional vacation, this is it for me." I'd work here, live here and, God willing, die here too.

"Ever get married?" I asked, for no other reason than I wanted to know.

Maybe most women would take offense to the blunt question, but not Gemma. She faced me and leaned a hip against the counter. "No. You?"

I shook my head. "No."

"Girlfriend?"

"Not presently." I took a sip of my beer, drinking in the liquid and her gorgeous hazel eyes. "I don't have time for a girlfriend."

"Because you're so busy with work."

"Yeah. As the assistant manager," I muttered.

She threw her head back and laughed, the musical sound stirring something in my chest. Making the urge to stand even stronger.

Gemma set her wine aside to snap some pasta in half and put them in a pot of boiling water. Then she crossed the room, floating with an easy grace, to curl up in the chair beside the couch. "What's happening with the ranch these days?"

"Same old. We're always wishing for rain and good cattle prices. The resort has grown these past few years—Kat gets a lot of credit for that—which adds a level of complexity. More staff, more guests, more problems. But we're getting into a good groove. Mostly, my headaches come from men with the last name Greer."

"Jake and JR."

"Yeah." It wasn't something I'd confided to anyone but

Cash in so many words. But talking with Gemma, despite how she frustrated and baited me, was surprisingly easy. She listened. She wouldn't play mediator like my family members and try to fix the problem.

Sometimes, all I really wanted was a person who listened.

"They don't want to let go," I said. "And I wish I could say I didn't understand, but when a place is your whole life, when you've given it everything year after year, I get it. It's just . . ."

"It's your turn."

"I want to build upon their legacy. I want to take the ranch and the resort a step further and be able to give that to the next generation. It's hard when they don't want to let go. When no one bothers to ask your opinion and when you make a decision, it's under a microscope."

"Makes sense. When I sold my company, the new owners asked me if I'd stay on for a year and act as interim CEO. But I knew I'd hate it. I wasn't going to answer to someone else's rules when I'd been making them for so long."

"So what would you do if you were me?"

She ran a finger around the rim of her glass. "I don't think you want my answer."

No, I was pretty sure I did. "Tell me."

"If this was my home, if this was my family, I'd thank my lucky stars that I had a grandfather and a father who were still trying to give what they have to offer because they'd rather die than see me fail."

"Well, fuck."

Gemma laughed. "I told you that you didn't want my answer."

"No, you're right." I sighed. "You're completely right and I hate it." Because I wasn't going to fail. And if I did, they'd be there to pick me up.

"I can empathize where you're coming from," she said. "And in your shoes, I'd feel the same. But you're talking to someone whose mother thought the next generation was there to service her boyfriends when they'd grown bored with her."

The beer bottle nearly slipped from my fingers. "What?"

"I don't know why I said that." Gemma flew out of the chair and returned to the kitchen.

She left me speechless while she ran.

But this time, Boston wasn't an option. And in a cabin of this size, there just wasn't far for her to go.

Was this her coping mechanism? She shut down and shut people out. She shoved them away. Was that why she'd left eleven years ago? Because I'd made her feel? Because here, she'd have a family who wouldn't have let her brush the past under a rug. Had she been hiding in her work ever since?

I set my bottle aside and walked to the kitchen as she furiously stirred the simmering sauce. "Gemma."

"Please forget I said that."

I crowded in close and tucked that lock of hair behind her ear. "Can't do that, darlin'."

She set the spoon down and looked at me with pleading eyes. "I don't like to talk about my mother or that part of my life. I spent years in therapy, and on my last session, I swore I didn't need to talk about it again. I really don't know why that slipped out."

"We don't have to talk about it." My hand fit perfectly around the nape of her neck. "But I'm here if you change your mind."

"Thanks." The tension eased from her shoulders as I skimmed my thumb over the skin beneath her ear.

I'd only meant to touch her for a second. To show her I was here and nothing more. But there was no such thing as a touch when it came to this woman. A zing raced beneath my skin. Electricity crackled between us and that pull, the gravity that surrounded her, sucked me right in. My hand trailed down her spine and her lips were so close that all I had to do was take them.

Gemma shivered, leaning in to my touch, as her gaze dropped to my mouth. Her tongue darted out and wet her bottom lip.

Then the pot of noodles boiled over. The hiss of the water hitting the burner broke us apart.

I dropped my hand and took a step back as Gemma fumbled for the dial to shut off the gas.

"This is probably about ready," she said.

"I'll set the table." And take a minute to get my head on straight.

Christ, I should have stayed on the couch.

The plates weren't in the same cupboard where Grandma had always kept them, and the silverware was in a different drawer. Admitting that Gemma's layout of the kitchen was more functional would only confirm out loud that she was fitting in, making this place her home, so I kept it to myself.

I heaped a pile of noodles onto my plate and smothered them in sauce and dug in. "This is great."

"It's actually your mother's recipe."

"Sauce from a jar with some embellishments? She tried to teach me but I never get the embellishments right and end up with just sauce from the jar."

Gemma smiled, twirling a string of noodles around her fork. "When I was here before, your mom was covering for the cook one day. There was this nasty cold running around, so there weren't many of us to feed. Londyn, Katherine and I were healthy—I always thought the junkyard gave us immune systems of steel—so we went to the kitchen to help her."

I leaned back in my chair, taking her in as she spoke because she captivated that kind of attention.

You set your silverware down for a woman like Gemma Lane.

"She taught us how to make her spaghetti," she said. "It was the first time anyone had ever taught me to cook."

"It's delicious. As good as hers. Do you cook often?"

"No." She shook her head. "I worked. And it's sort of depressing to cook for one person every night."

"I can relate." I went back to my meal, the two of us eating without much conversation.

When my plate was clear, I leaned deeper into my chair, making no move to leave. There wasn't anywhere else I wanted to be at the moment. The only thing waiting for me at home was the television and a massive pile of laundry. And Gemma's company was addictive.

"Want to know the real reason I left Boston?" she asked.

She'd told me it was because she'd sold her company and had wanted a change of scenery, but I'd wondered lately if that was only a half-truth. "Yeah."

"I didn't feel anything about my life." She lifted a shoulder, like she was just as confused as I was why she was telling me these things. Then she dropped her gaze, hiding the emotion in her eyes by toying with the uneaten spaghetti on her plate.

I didn't blink. I didn't breathe. I didn't move for fear that she'd stop talking.

"I don't know when I went numb. I used to feel things." She looked up and forced a too-bright smile. "Anger or annoyance or excitement. On the day I was approached about selling Gemma Lane, that idea hadn't even crossed my mind. I don't even know why I entertained it, but I was eating lunch with an old colleague and she asked me if I was sick."

"Were you?"

"I don't get sick." She shook her head. "It took me a minute to figure out what she was talking about. But then I realized she thought I was tired. And I wasn't. I really wasn't. I was just . . . empty."

"Maybe you were ready for a career change."

She shook her head. "A life change. It wasn't just work. I was dating this guy and he'd asked me to marry him."

A flare of jealousy raced through my veins, but I set it aside.

"Obviously, I said no." She wiggled the bare fingers on her left hand. "So I had this friend who thought I was sick. A man who wanted to share his life with me, but instead I broke his heart. And it all came together and made me pause. I looked over the past year and realized that I was going day after day and I didn't feel . . . anything."

Her eyes turned glassy, but she held tight, not letting a tear fall.

I stretched my hand across the table and covered hers. "Gem."

"I don't want to live like that." She flipped her hand over so our palms were pressed together and stared at them, my wide hand nearly covering her long fingers.

"And since you got here? Feel anything?"

Her eyes flashed to mine. "Some days."

"Besides frustration with me?"

A smile spread across her stunning face. "Maybe."

"Good." A surge of pride swelled in my chest because I'd done that. Me. I'd put that smile there and it was mine. "Glad I could piss you off."

"Among other things." She laughed and slipped her hand free, then collected our plates and took them to the sink.

"Want some help washing up?"

"I've got it. Want another beer?"

"Better not."

If I stayed, I wouldn't leave. We'd put the fighting aside tonight, and we both knew this was heading toward dangerous territory. She was in a strange emotional place and I knew nothing would change.

Gemma would stay until Christmas, mostly because I'd dared her. Partly because she wanted to. Then she'd head to California, leaving me behind.

I'd spend another eleven years wondering what had become of Gemma.

I stood from the table. "Thanks for dinner."

"Thanks for staying. And for the firewood."

"See ya." I went to the door to tug on my boots. Then I opened the door before I decided kissing her was worth another eleven-year wait.

CHAPTER NINE

GEMMA

The moment he opened the door, I chased after him. "Easton, wait."

"Yeah?"

I crossed the room, not caring that the cold night air was chasing away the fire's warmth and stepped into his space.

Standing before him in my bare feet, his tall, strong body shrouded mine. He made me feel small—safe and protected. He made me feel free to be myself.

Easton made me feel. Period.

I wasn't ready for him to go and take the feeling with him. Not yet. Not when I'd been numb for so long and with him here, I was alive.

"I'm sorry."

His forehead furrowed. "For what?"

"For leaving like I did. After that night, I shouldn't

have snuck away without a goodbye."

"It's fine." His gaze was unreadable. "We were young. It was just a hookup."

Except it hadn't been a hookup.

Easton had been my first.

Not that I'd been a virgin, but he'd been the one *I'd* chosen. Me.

When I was fourteen and still living at home, I'd lost my virginity to a guy who'd worked as a clerk at the gas station close to my neighborhood. I'd ridden my bike over to get away from my mother for a few hours. I'd gone in to use the bathroom and he'd stopped me on the way out. He'd asked if I wanted a case of beer, offering to sell it to me even though he'd known I hadn't been twenty-one.

I'd picked wine instead because my mother served her boyfriends beer. And they were trash. I was going to be classy and that meant drinking wine—or it had to my fourteen-year-old brain. The boy had sold it to me, and I'd stayed at the gas station drinking while he'd finished his Saturday shift.

Then, in a dark alley that had smelled like garbage, I'd let him take my virginity in the backseat of his car.

That boy hadn't been my choice. Yes, I'd picked him, but not because I'd been attracted to him or liked him or could remember his name. I'd picked him simply so I could *give* my virginity, not have it taken. I'd been terrified that eventually one of the men Mom had brought around would take me against my will.

I knew that eventually, one of them wouldn't be satisfied when she made me watch or when she made me touch.

But Easton, he'd been mine.

He'd been the first man I'd desired.

There'd been countless nights since when I'd remember the feel of being in his arms and how he'd held me. How he'd kissed me with tenderness and how he'd cherished my body.

The morning I'd left his bed, before the sun had risen, my footsteps had never been heavier.

Easton had been so good to me. He'd set the standard for future men in my life and not one had measured up.

No, it hadn't been a hookup.

That night had been my everything.

"Hookup or not, thank you." I placed a hand over his heart. "That night meant a lot to me."

Easton studied me, trying to figure out where this was coming from. Maybe he'd eventually figure me out, as it seemed like he was trying.

Maybe if he did, he could clue me in because I was as fucked up now as I'd been at sixteen.

My hand rose and fell with the rise of his chest. My fingers looked tiny compared to the breadth of his shoulders. Through the cotton of his shirt, his heart pulsed in steady beats and the heat of his skin warmed mine. I let the spark between us sink deep into my veins.

Easton covered my hand with one of his, trapping me to him. "What do you want, Gem?"

A place.

A safe place. A forever place.

Maybe that place didn't exist for women like me, so I stood on my toes, threw my free arm around his shoulders and brushed my lips against his before I gave him my second choice. "You."

He didn't hesitate. Easton crushed his lips to mine, letting my hand go so both arms could snake around me. The heat from his body spread like fire, racing through my body and stealing my breath.

I gasped as he lifted me off my toes and took one long stride into the cabin, kicking the door closed behind us with his boot.

His tongue swept inside my mouth, twisting and tangling with mine, as a rush of desire pooled in my core. The erection beneath his jeans dug into my hip and his hard length only increased the frenzy.

I was needy. Aching. Melting into his strong body. I latched on to his bottom lip, sucking it into my mouth as my arms clung to him.

"Stop." He broke his mouth away, panting. "Are you sure?"

"If you walk out that door without fucking me, I'll never speak to you again."

The corner of his mouth turned up. "Promise?"

I laughed and leaned in to take his earlobe between

my teeth. "Easton. Fuck me."

"Whatever you say, darlin'." His mouth latched on to the skin of my neck and he spun us toward the living room but stopped after two steps. "Wait. Damn it. I don't have a condom."

I pointed over his shoulder to the coat rack. "Purse."

Easton spun us again, growling against my skin as he walked. His hands dropped to my ass, palming it with those large hands before setting me down so I could yank my purse off the hook and dig.

His chest hit my back and his lips found the sensitive spot beneath my ear. The caress of his breath and the wet warmth of his tongue dizzied my brain and I swayed on my feet. His arms banded around me, and one hand cupped my breast as the other went for the button on my jeans.

"Hustle up," he commanded.

I was struggling to keep a grip on my purse, let alone search through it in the hopes that I'd find the condom I carried for emergency purposes.

When I couldn't feel it in the interior pocket, I started throwing things onto the floor. Lip glosses. Pens. A packet of gum. I ripped items out in a flurry, just wanting to find my goddamn wallet as Easton tortured me with his lips and hands.

My nipples were pebbled inside my bra and when he slipped a hand underneath my sweater, raking those calloused fingers up my ribs, I began to quiver.

"Gemma. Condom."

I snapped back to reality, clinging to the last thread of my focus to search for my wallet. When I had it in my hand, I threw my twelve-thousand-dollar handbag on the floor and ripped open the flap of the matching wallet.

My finger hit the foil packet at the exact moment Easton's slid into my panties and found my clit.

"Oh my God." I sagged against him, letting him hold me up as my eyes fell closed. "East, I . . ." My ability to speak and form coherent sentences disappeared as he toyed with me, playing me with those expert fingers.

"Come." His gravelly voice tickled my skin as two of his fingers slid inside. "Come on my fingers."

I managed a nod before a surge of heat spread through my limbs. Ecstasy consumed every nerve ending until I bucked against his hand and detonated. My orgasm was hard and fast and so fucking satisfying. I was still riding the high when he slid both his hands free and spun me around, catching me before I could topple to the floor.

Easton shuffled me backward until my back hit the wall. He took my chin in a hand and tipped it up, holding me exactly where he wanted me as his mouth crashed onto mine.

My palm flattened against his zipper, rubbing his arousal through the denim. He groaned down my throat, pressing deeper into my touch. Then his hand released my jaw so he could use both hands to strip the jeans off my hips.

I kicked them off as he took a fistful of my lace panties and shredded them off my body.

"Open it." He nodded to the condom I'd managed to keep in my fingers. Then the sound of metal scraping metal filled my ears as he flicked the clasp on his oval belt buckle. The sound of his zipper opening came next.

"Holy fuck." My eyes bulged as his thick length bobbed free. He'd been wearing nothing under those jeans the entire time. No boxers or briefs. Just Easton Greer going commando as he'd sat at my small table eating spaghetti.

Too distracted by the sight of his cock, I nearly dropped the condom. He snatched it from me before it fell from my fingers and put the foil between his teeth to rip it open and sheath himself.

Then I was up, his hands lifting me in the air with a swift bounce before he spread my legs wide and thrust inside.

"Ah," I gasped, stretching around him as he fell forward, cursing and groaning into my neck. "Move."

He shook his head.

"East, move." I dug my nails into his back, clawing through his shirt. That earned me a nip on my jaw as he slid out only to push inside again, this time going even deeper.

My entire body shivered.

"Fuck, that feels good."

I hummed my agreement as he slid in and out once

more.

We moved in tandem, his hips rolling forward as I leveraged the wall to meet his strokes. The sound of slapping skin and labored breathing filled the room. He kept his eyes locked on mine, that intense gaze boring into mine with every move. Easton held me captive, pinned and at his mercy.

The build of my second orgasm was slower than the first, but it didn't take Easton long to bring me to the breaking point. Sparks pooled and I felt—I felt everything —as I toppled over the edge. The explosion was devastating. He shattered me completely, leaving me in tiny pieces that would never fit together in the same way again.

"Christ, Gem," he whispered, leaning into me as I clenched around him, pulse after endless pulse, until he moaned into my ear and shuddered with his own release.

I collapsed into him as we both came down, my arms limp and boneless as I gave him my weight. My ponytail had come loose and my hair was draped around us. My ankles were locked around his back and my cashmere sweater was likely ruined from this encounter with a log wall.

Much like with my French lace panties, I couldn't find the energy to care.

With a kiss to my temple, Easton eased me to my feet, holding my elbow as I found my balance. "Good?"

I nodded and shoved my hair out of my face. "I'm good."

"Be back." He pulled his jeans up to cover his ass, the zipper and the belt hanging loose, as he disappeared down the hallway to the bathroom.

I blinked away the fog and searched for my jeans. I stepped into them and had them buttoned as he emerged.

Jeans zipped. Belt fastened. Shirt tucked.

His eyes flickered between me and the door.

"So . . ." I picked up the scrap of fabric formerly known as my underwear.

"I'm not good at this," he admitted, raking a hand through the hair I'd tousled at some point. "The after."

The after? Oh. After a hookup. *Right.*

"Then let's skip it. Goodnight, Easton."

He sighed and walked toward the door, hesitating for a moment like he was going to come over and kiss me. But he didn't. He twisted the knob, tipped his chin and said, "Goodnight, Gemma."

———

"HEY." I knocked on Katherine's open office door.

"Hey. Are you done for today?"

"Yep." I took my usual chair, the one I sat in every afternoon at this time. "My relief has arrived."

Annabeth had hired a local high school girl to work the desk after school each evening. It was a great hire for the long-term resort staff. For me, it meant that after four o'clock, I had nothing to do but go to the cabin. Alone.

"Want to have dinner?" I asked.

"I can't tonight." Katherine rolled her eyes. "I have a town council meeting."

"Well, look at you. You're on the town council."

She shrugged. "I took a seat after Liddy stepped down last year. Rain check?"

"Sure." I smiled, wishing I had her jam-packed schedule like the one I used to have in Boston.

Because if I had meetings and appointments each night, I wouldn't go home and dwell on the fact that I'd had sex with Easton last night. I'd already spent the day overthinking it.

What had I been thinking? How was I supposed to be around him now? How was I supposed to act during family dinner or when he came into the lodge or when I ran into him outside?

Had that just been another one of his hookups? Did he do that with other people at the resort? There were some pretty girls who worked here. I'd seen them coming and going as they worked. In a way, they reminded me of Katherine, Londyn and me at that stage. Had any of them caught Easton's eye? Had any of them begged him for a riding lesson?

Bitches.

"Okay, what's wrong?" Katherine asked.

I blinked. "Huh?"

"I don't know where you were right then, but the look on your face was murderous."

I groaned and folded forward, dropping my face into my hands. "I had sex with Easton."

"What?" Katherine shrieked. "When?"

"Last night." I cringed. "And . . . eleven years ago."

"Sit up and spill."

I obeyed. "He came over last night to deliver firewood. I asked him to stay for dinner and . . . sex." Incredible. Unforgettable. Wild sex.

"You're blushing, Gemma," she teased.

I covered my cheeks with my hands. "He's . . . well, you've seen him. He's gorgeous and infuriating and overwhelming."

"So last night. What about eleven years ago?"

"It was the night before I left. He was living in one of the apartments beside the staff quarters, remember?"

"Yeah. I took his apartment when he moved out." She scrunched up her nose. "Eww. You had sex in my bed."

I giggled. "Sorry."

She waved it off. "Continue."

"I was outside watching the sunset. And he found me."

Easton hadn't known it at the time, but I'd been outside watching the sunset and memorizing the line of the mountains since I'd been ready to leave. And for the first time, he hadn't given me a chin jerk and kept on walking. He'd stopped, leaned against the same fence rail, and stared at the horizon.

We hadn't talked much. He'd asked me if I liked it here.

I'd told him the truth.

Yes.

I'd always loved the Greer Ranch.

But that hadn't stopped me from leaving.

"We stayed outside until after sunset. When he escorted me inside, he had this look. Like he wanted to invite me into his room, but he wasn't sure I'd say yes. It was the first time I'd seen just a tiny crack in that confidence of his. So I kissed him."

I'd spent the night in his bed until he'd fallen asleep, and then I'd snuck out. Before the sunrise, I'd walked the miles to the highway and had hitchhiked my way to Missoula. Then I'd hopped on a bus and left for Boston.

"That explains why he was such a grumpy bastard those months after you left," Katherine said. "I always thought it was because he was mad at you on my behalf. Which was sort of sweet, in a big brother way."

"Oh, I'm sure that was part of it too. He loves you."

"Like a sister. They all love me like a sister." The light dimmed in her eyes for a split second before a smile spread across her pretty face. "Is this a bad time to remind you that we have a no-fraternization policy for employees?"

I picked up a paperclip from her desk and threw it at her head. "You're not helping!"

She laughed. "Sorry. What are you going to do about him?"

"I have no idea. He's . . . complicated."

The attraction between us was this steady charge, this undercurrent impossible to ignore. If we weren't at each other's throats, fighting, it was futile and well . . . that had led to us fucking against the cabin wall.

"What would you do?" I asked.

"Talk to him. He's dealing with a lot right now and he's supposed to be in charge, but people forget to *talk* to him. They forget to ask what he thinks or how he feels."

I loved my friend. And I loved her even more for seeing Easton's struggles when everyone else around here seemed oblivious.

It wasn't my place to decide how to proceed after last night—Katherine was right. I'd made that decision last time by leaving and had taken Easton's choice away.

I wouldn't make the same mistake twice.

So three hours later, I drove the Cadillac to his house.

It was dark outside because I'd waited until after dinner before getting in my car. I hadn't wanted to get here and have him still be working somewhere on the ranch. Katherine had written down directions to his place, and I'd held the sticky note in one hand while I drove with the other.

I'd had to drive away from the lodge and across the highway, to a section of the Greers' property that wasn't used for the resort. This was pure ranch country with open meadows bordered by groves of trees and barbed wire fences. The gravel road to his home followed a wandering stream, and when his house came into view, it stole my breath.

The house was centered in the field with the mountains rising up in the distance. The roofline matched almost exactly to the highest peak on the horizon. Golden light flooded through the abundant windows, beckoning me closer. The umber wood siding matched the other buildings on the ranch.

The home, commanding in size and stature, made a bold statement yet fit absolutely in its natural surroundings. It was exactly what I'd expected from Easton, yet surprising at the same time because of its sheer elegance.

The garage door was open as I pulled into the driveway and Easton came outside with a red rag in his grip.

My heart fluttered, seeing him in a pair of jeans and simple white T-shirt. Stubble dusted his jaw and his hair was mussed from a long day's work. A dull throb pulsed between my legs at the sight of him. Damn, he was hot.

Was he wearing boxers today? Or was he going commando again?

I'd come here with the intention of talking and talking only, but if he showed even the slightest interest, I was going to break that plan.

I sat in my car, parked, but unable to shut it off and get out. I simply stared at him through the windshield.

And he stared back.

Easton broke first, a frown crossing his handsome face

as he planted his fists on his hips in a silent ultimatum. Was I coming or going?

Coming.

I sucked in a deep breath and shut off the car, stepping outside into the cold and hurrying toward the garage. "Hey."

He looked me up and down. "Where's your coat?"

"I need to buy one. I was supposed to be in California in October, not Montana."

He stomped into the garage and hit the button to close the door behind us. "What are you doing here?"

"I thought we'd better talk about last night."

"Why?"

Why? Seriously? "Because I thought you might have an opinion about what happened and you're the one who said he wished other people would consider his opinions. But hey, if I'm wrong and you just want to forget it ever happened and go back to treating me like shit beneath your boot, I'll stay out of your way until Christmas."

I wanted to turn and march to my car, but he'd trapped me inside. The only way out of the garage was through the button at his back, so I crossed my arms and shot him my best glare.

He ran a hand through that thick hair, then stalked my way.

I'd worn a scarf over the only coat I'd packed—a black leather jacket. Easton unwrapped the scarf from my neck. "Sorry."

"I'm not here to fight with you."

Easton tossed the scarf on the cement floor. It was as clean as the floor in the cabin. His hands skimmed my arms, sliding over the buttery Italian leather, until they came to my face. "I don't want to fight either."

His mouth dropped to mine, erasing the trace of irritation and replacing it with a burning lust that had me pushing the hem of his shirt above his ribs.

"Inside," I panted against his lips, tugging his belt buckle free. I wanted him in a bed and the chance to do this all night long.

Easton shook his head and walked me to the workbench that ran the length of the garage. I opened my mouth to protest, but then I was lost in an oblivion of Easton's mouth and hands and body. When I walked out of the garage an hour later on wobbly legs, I had a smile on my face, his scent on my skin and his taste on my tongue.

I was sated. For the first time in years, I didn't feel the urge to move on to the next thing. I didn't have work or a task to tackle. I could just enjoy the moment.

And I did, for the first five minutes of my drive home. Then I replayed the night. And last night.

Easton and I had fucked twice. Hard. Both times, he'd screwed me on the closest available surface. Maybe he'd been as desperate for me as I'd been for him.

Or maybe my mother had been right from the start.

Maybe I would always be just another cheap thrill.

CHAPTER TEN

GEMMA

Avoiding a man who worked and lived in the same place you did wasn't an easy feat, but somehow, I'd managed to dodge Easton for three days.

Or maybe he'd been dodging me.

Other than a glimpse of him riding Jigsaw away from the stables yesterday, I hadn't seen hide nor hair of him since the night I'd driven away from his house. He'd looked incredible on that horse. His breath had billowed in a cloud around him—so had Jigsaw's—and he'd been wearing a heavy canvas coat, cowboy hat with the brim tipped low and leather chaps laced up his long legs.

Easton had perfected sexy, mysterious cowboy. The man belonged on the cover of a romance novel—shirtless, of course.

His mouthwatering appeal was the reason avoidance had become necessary.

When he was around, I couldn't think clearly and I was in need of some unmuddied thinking.

Either I could lean into this, soak him up until it was time to move on, or I ended it now.

My brain was lobbying for option two. It would be easy to retreat to the robot I'd been in Boston. But my heart was struggling to get on board. Because damn it, here I was, living, breathing and feeling for the first time in a long time, and it was a rush.

Then again, a numb heart didn't hurt when it was broken.

It was Friday and the Greers were expecting me for family dinner, but the idea of sitting beside Easton, pretending that I hadn't had him inside me twice this week . . . well, that wasn't an option.

So I'd begged Katherine to make my excuses and because Carol was the type to come track me down at the cabin, I'd done what all grown-ups would do.

I got the hell off Greer property.

The moment my shift at the lodge had ended, I climbed in the Cadillac and drove into Clear River. Shopping at the small, local grocery store hadn't taken me as long as I'd hoped. When there were only seven aisles, it didn't take a long time to go up and down each. Twice.

So after loading up my foodstuffs, I'd decided to stop for a drink at the Clear River Bar.

I wasn't the only one in need of a cocktail, judging by the crowded parking lot.

Trucks of varying makes and models had taken all but three open spaces. I eased the Cadillac in between a white Ford and a filthy black Chevy, then got out and hit the locks. A chocolate lab sitting shotgun in the Chevy stared me down as country music filled the air. The bar's windows were crowded with neon beer signs, and the red tin siding had faded under years of brutal sunshine. A plastic, camo banner had been tied to the front of the building, advertising HUNTERS WELCOME in bright orange letters.

The smell of beer and stale cigarettes assaulted my nostrils when I opened the door and my eyes took a few moments to adjust to the dim light. Conversation seemed to halt as the whole room turned in their stools and chairs.

The bar was situated along one side of the room, and as I crossed the scuffed tile floor, heading for one of the only empty stools, most faces followed my path. I'd never felt so many eyes on my ass in my life.

Maybe a drink was a mistake.

It was only when I was on a stool, ass hidden, that the dull drum of conversation resumed, merging with the jukebox's music from the corner.

"What can I get you?" the bartender asked, setting out a paper coaster. Besides me, she was the only female in the room.

"Do you have wine?"

She looked me up and down, leaning in to lower her

voice. "Were you looking for the resort? Because I think you might be lost."

"Nope, not headed for the resort."

"Then you'll be disappointed. All I have is a box of Franzia, vintage last month."

I laughed. "Then how about a vodka soda with lemon?"

"That I can handle." She smiled, then went to the other end of the bar, talking to a few other patrons while she mixed my drink. When she brought it back, she snagged a menu off the stack. "Cheeseburgers are on special tonight if you're hungry."

"Sold."

"Fries?"

I nodded. "Please."

"You got it." She returned to her end of the bar, leaving me alone.

The two guys next to me were wrapped up in their conversation about politics and paid me no attention as I twirled the red straw in my glass, clinking the ice cubes and poking the lemon wedge. I sipped my drink slowly as I took in the room.

A lot of eyes flickered my way but none lingered too long. The man on the stool exactly opposite mine finished his beer, shook hands with the guy at his side, then waved goodbye to the bartender. As he opened the door to leave, another figure appeared beyond him.

His cowboy hat dipped as he exchanged greetings, then my stomach dropped.

Because I knew that hat.

Son of a bitch. How was I supposed to avoid Easton in a bar this size? Wasn't he supposed to be at dinner?

He walked inside, scanning the room and lifting a hand to wave at a few tables. Then he walked to the bar, taking off his hat as he pulled out the stool that had just been vacated. He greeted the guy directly on his left, then grinned at the bartender as she approached.

Easton's gaze drifted past her and when he spotted me, the grin dropped.

Ouch.

I lifted my glass, giving him a silent salute.

Easton acknowledged me with a single nod.

My heart was in my throat as I took another drink, wishing I hadn't ordered that cheeseburger. Wishing I was in any other seat than this where I had no choice but see him when I faced forward.

How was I supposed to avoid that strong jaw and those dark, dreamy eyes when they were *right there?*

"Here you go." The bartender emerged from the kitchen with a plastic basket lined with parchment paper. At least I wouldn't have to wait long for my meal. The cheeseburger was bigger than my face and the heap of fries was the equivalent of three extra-large potatoes. "Hope you're hungry."

I had been. "Thanks."

I cut the burger in half as she returned to her post, leaning a hip against the bar as she focused all her attention on one man.

Easton.

I kept my eyes on my meal, but the claw of jealousy scraped deeper every time I heard her laugh carry over the music. Or when I'd catch his smile from the corner of my eye. I was chewing with rabid fury when she leaned in closer to whisper something in his ear.

He laughed. She laughed.

She smiled. He smiled.

I was most definitely not laughing or smiling.

No, I was his latest conquest, and he'd waited a whole three days before moving on to someone else. Or maybe go back for another round with a former lover.

She was gorgeous and fresh faced. Her blond hair brushed the tops of her shoulders in effortless, beach waves. Her tee dipped low enough to show a hint of cleavage and she had the perfect hourglass figure, curves I'd only dreamt of having.

But it was her smile that I envied most. It was carefree and effortless. A pretty smile. One that made Easton smile too, wider than I'd seen since arriving in Montana.

He didn't smile around me, not like that. And as I'd suspected, it was devastating.

"Hey, sweetheart."

I jerked, forcing my eyes away from Easton and the bartender as a man leaned against the bar at my side.

"How's it going?" he asked.

"Fantastic," I deadpanned, not in the mood to deal with stranger small talk and a guy who likely saw me as fresh meat.

He'd brought a beer along from wherever he'd emerged and tipped it to his lips as he grinned. "New in town or just visiting."

"Visiting." I ate another bite, busying my mouth so I didn't have to talk, and cast a glance toward Easton.

His gaze was waiting, the tension in his jaw visible as he squeezed his own beer bottle to death.

For a moment, I thought he might come over, but then the bartender stood in front of him, giving Easton an eye-level shot of her generous breasts.

My appetite vanished and I tossed the uneaten portion of my burger into the tray, wiping my hands and lips with a napkin. Then I dove for my wallet, ripping out a hundred-dollar bill and slapping it on the bar.

I wasn't sure how much a burger and a cocktail cost in Clear River, Montana, but that should cover it.

"Leaving already?" the man asked.

Not bothering with the obvious answer, I slipped the strap of my purse over my shoulder and—eyes forward—I walked out of the bar and into the fading evening light.

In a way, I should be happy he'd come to the bar. That he'd flirted with another woman in front of me. I'd been conflicted over what to do with Easton, but tonight had been eye-opening.

This was not the place for me.

Easton was not the man for me. As much as I liked my little cabin, I didn't fit here. He'd been right all along.

I didn't fit.

Spending three months here wouldn't change that fact. Bet or not, I was leaving. He could gloat to his family while I was a thousand miles south, enjoying some California sunshine.

I'd stick around long enough to spend a few more nights with Katherine. But as soon as the groceries in my trunk were gone, so was I.

The light was nearly gone by the time I made it home to the cabin. The stars were out in full force and the temperature was dropping fast. Before unloading the Cadillac, I made a fire to warm up the cabin, then I busied myself with putting groceries away.

There was enough food here for a week. I'd invite Katherine over as often as possible and the two of us would have a bit more time together before I hit the road. If I was lucky, the weather would hold out and I wouldn't get snowed in.

By the time the groceries were unloaded, the cabin was toasty warm and I poured myself a hearty glass of wine, lifting my glass to the empty room. "Cheers to another week. And a lonely Friday night."

Tears flooded my eyes, and before I could pull them in, I was crying off my makeup.

This wasn't why I'd come to Montana. This wasn't why I'd started this journey.

I wanted to feel, but this? *No, thank you.*

But the dam had broken and there was no holding back the flood. Drops of ugly poured from my body in a stream of uncontrollable tears and broken sobs.

I stood there, in the middle of the room with my wine sloshing over the rim of my glass and cried.

I cried for the life I'd worked so hard to build. The life that had meant so fucking much to me three months ago. The life I'd left behind.

Selling the company and leaving Boston hadn't been a mistake, but for the first time, I mourned. Because twelve million dollars in the bank hadn't made me any less alone.

The tears came faster. The sobs wracked harder. My knees were seconds from giving way, collapsing me into a pathetic puddle, when two arms wrapped around me and kept me from falling.

Easton pinned me to his chest, holding me with one arm as he took the wine from my hand and set it on the table beside us. Then he let me soak the front of his green shirt with my tears.

I held tight, letting him keep me standing, because I couldn't seem to pull it together. No matter how many deep breaths I sucked in through my nose, they exhaled in a mess. Until finally, minutes later, one of them stuck. Then another. And the tears just . . . ran out.

Even when I stopped crying, Easton didn't let me go.

"I'm okay." I pushed him away and wiped my face dry, turning my back to him because he'd witnessed rock bottom. "Sorry."

"What was that, Gem?"

"Nothing." I waved him off. "What are you doing here?"

"You left the bar upset."

Honestly, I was surprised he'd noticed. And that he'd come to check on me. Or maybe he was here for a hookup. Regardless, I was such a train wreck that I hadn't even heard him drive up. "It's nothing. Sometimes women cry."

"Bullshit. What the hell is going on?"

"Nothing. It's been a long week."

"Gemma." He took my elbow and spun me to face him.

"What!" I batted his hand away. "It's nothing."

He stood there, unwavering, and leveled me with a look that said he had no intention of leaving until he got his answer.

The stubborn ass. "You were flirting with the bartender."

"Liz?" He barked a laugh. "I don't flirt with Liz. She's been my friend since we were in diapers."

"That was flirting. You smiled at her. You were laughing and whispering."

"Yeah, she told me the guy three seats down smelled like cheese. I laughed because she's funny and easy to hang out with."

Long-time friend or not, I didn't want to hear about how much he enjoyed another woman's company. "You don't laugh with me."

"You're not funny."

I poked him in the pec. "I'm being serious."

He scowled and rubbed the spot where I'd jabbed him. "So am I. Say something funny and I'll laugh."

"But I'm not funny." The tears came again and this time, they just made me angry. "Goddamn it!"

He shook his head, coming closer as I furiously wiped my eyes dry. "You were jealous."

"Yes," I admitted. "I have some issues when it comes to men."

"Let's get one thing straight." He clasped my shoulders, looming and waiting until he had my undivided attention. "There are no *men*. There's one man. Me. And if you have an issue with me, we'll sure as fuck talk it through."

I dropped my head into my hands, the shame no doubt showing on my face. "Sorry."

Easton took my wrists and pulled them away. "Should we talk about why you've been avoiding me this week?"

"You wouldn't take me to your bed." Apparently, there was no stopping the truth flood tonight.

"Huh?"

"You screwed me against the wall." I flicked my wrist, motioning to said wall. "And made me come on that bench in your garage."

"Three times."

"Three times." I rolled my eyes. "But you wouldn't take me to your bedroom."

He shook his head, blinking as he tried to make heads or tails of my nonsense. I didn't blame him for the confused look on his face.

"Ugh. Never mind." I threw my hands in the air. "I'm losing my fucking mind. Welcome to the mixed-up world of Gemma Lane. This actually feels like your fault. What are you doing to me?"

"The same thing you're doing to me," he grumbled. "Driving me fucking insane."

I laughed.

It wasn't funny but it was funny.

"I worked so hard to not be crazy. To not be my mother. I left her house and decided I would never be out of control again. I'd prove that I was better. So I worked hard and showed the world—myself—that I would never be her. I succeeded. I am a millionaire. I am in control of my destiny, and I am not the person she tried to make me. I am not *her*."

"You're not her."

I shook my head. "No."

There was a comfort in saying it out loud. And for the moment, that was enough to soothe some of my jagged edges.

Mortifying as it was, I was glad the person here to witness it was Easton.

"I'm sorry," I said again. "Forget about all of this. Please."

"I can't do that." He lifted his hand and cupped my cheek. "You said you don't want to talk about it. I get that. But this is the second time you've cracked the door to your past, darlin'. I think it's time to open up and let me in."

"It doesn't matter. The whole point of this rant is that I might be having a crazy moment, but my mother was certifiably insane. No one rescued me from her. So I rescued myself. And part of that meant shutting out the world. But here things are so . . . different. I can't hide from you in my work. I don't have work. I wanted to feel things and here I am, feeling again. It's an adjustment."

He studied my face, his eyes softening. "That goes both ways. You're all I've thought about for three days and I know the smartest thing for me to do would be to walk out that door. But . . ."

"But what?" I whispered as his thumb traced a line of tingles on my skin.

"But I'm going to take you into the bedroom and make sure you know that the reason I fucked you against that wall and in my garage was not because you don't deserve the bedroom." He bent and brushed his lips against mine. "But because when it comes to you, I have no control."

CHAPTER ELEVEN

EASTON

"Morning, boss," Rory called from the hayloft before tossing a bale down. "You're here early."

"Rory, what are you doing here?"

"Oh, uh, Johnson called to see if I'd cover his shift today. He's sick or something."

Sick, my ass. Johnson didn't like Saturday mornings because he was usually at the bar too late on Friday nights. He'd probably shown up not long after I'd left to chase Gemma last night, then stayed until Liz kicked him out at two. This was the second time in a month I'd come to the stables on a Saturday expecting to see him and finding Rory instead.

If Johnson wasn't careful, I was going to fire him and give Rory a hefty raise.

Rory was due one anyway. He showed up on time and

worked hard. His attitude was unmatched. Hell, it was better than mine.

"When you're done up there, come on into my office."

"All right." He nodded and tossed down another bale.

I left him to his work and retreated to my office. The room was cold, so I turned up the baseboard heaters before shrugging off my coat. Then I eased the door closed to keep the warmth inside and settled in behind my desk.

Doing paperwork and checking emails was not my favorite task, let alone on a Saturday morning before seven, but after slipping out of Gemma's bed this morning, I hadn't wanted to go home.

She'd been out cold, her hair spread across the pillow and her face burrowed under the covers. I'd lit a fire to warm up the cabin, then driven away with the image of her sleeping peacefully in my mind.

Last night had been intense. Finding her sobbing, breaking down, had destroyed me. I knew she'd been embarrassed, not that there was anything to be ashamed of. And as much as I'd wanted to dive deeper into her past, the moment I'd kissed her, the chance to talk had flown out the window.

The two of us had spent the night exploring each other's bodies and the sex had been just as intense. She met my desire with a raging passion of her own.

That woman had me twisted as tight as the braid on a bullwhip.

So this morning, I escaped to the stables because the

distraction of work might be my only hope of getting my head on straight.

After the night Gemma had driven out to my house, I'd given her some space, not wanting to come on too strong. Last night, I'd begged out of family dinner because I hadn't wanted to make her uncomfortable in front of my family.

Maybe giving her that space had been a mistake.

But I was glad I'd found her at the bar.

Had I been flirting with Liz? I'd known her since we were kids. Her family was as local to this valley as mine. She was my friend. We'd shared a fumbling kiss sometime during middle school, but besides that, our relationship had always been platonic.

Liz touched my arm a lot, and she always hung out near my end of the bar when I was in, but did she have feelings for me?

No. No way. Liz didn't act anything like a woman who wanted me in her bed. She was a friend. Nothing more.

Gemma was the only woman who'd be tangled in my sheets.

She put on such a strong façade. She was fearless and wild. But beneath it all, she was scared. Of me. Of her future. She hid her fears well, but last night, I'd been given a glimpse. Would she run from those fears? Or would she stay here and face them?

Would she let me in?

Rory appeared in the door's window and I waved him

inside. He shrugged off the Carhartt coat he'd been wearing and hung it on the hook beside my own.

"Thanks for coming in today," I said.

"No problem. I like the hours."

I steepled my fingers in front of my chin and took a long look at the boy. Though he wasn't really a boy anymore. Maybe because I'd seen him grow up, I still saw him as the kid who'd chased Mom's border collie, Max, around the yard. But Rory stood nearly as tall as me at six three and if he kept working like he did, he'd fill out his lanky frame.

"I'm giving you a raise."

His jaw dropped. "You are?"

"An extra two dollars an hour." There was no need to wait on his raise. He'd earned it. And it was time to give him more responsibilities too. "I want you to start shadowing Cash in the afternoons when he's not on a ride. You're a natural with horses but I want you to get more experience with breaking the younger animals."

If this new horse facility worked out, Rory would be a good asset for Cash. It would suck to lose him here, but I wasn't going to cost the kid an opportunity at a better job because hiring stable hands was a pain in my ass.

"Okay." A grin stretched across his face. "You got it."

"Good. Focus on the stables this morning. Then I'd like you to take Oreo out for a long ride. Work him hard. Cash said he was a real shit the other day for one of the guests. Maybe he just needs to burn some energy and get a reminder about who's in charge."

"Will do." Rory stood from the chair and grabbed his coat but paused as he opened the door. "Thanks, Easton. I sure do appreciate the raise. And the opportunity."

"You've earned it."

He nodded, closing the door behind him and leaving me to my emails. There wasn't much for me to do on a regular basis in the office. Thankfully, our bookkeeper made sure the bills and employees were paid. It allowed me to be out where I needed to be, on the land with the animals and with the staff.

But there were days when desk work was unavoidable. The schedule needed to be drafted for next month so I could send it to Katherine. We'd have a three-hour meeting to pair my staff with her resort activities and guest needs. Then I'd fill in gaps to make sure all the ranch work was covered.

I rolled up my sleeves and dove in, putting in the couple of hours necessary to work it through, while I ate a few granola bars I kept stashed in my desk. After the schedule was penciled into the calendar, I fired up my computer and scrolled through the emails I'd been ignoring for the last week.

Most were deleted and I'd almost cleared through everything when the ding of an incoming message filled the room.

It was an email from my Realtor and I clicked it immediately to read the message.

"Yes." I fist-pumped and double-clicked the attachment. It was the same moment my phone rang. "Hey," I answered. "I just opened your email."

"Good," she said. "I wanted to call and make sure it came through and you didn't have any questions on the buy-sell."

"Seems straightforward." The sellers had accepted my offer with a few reasonable contingencies. Which meant it was time to tell my family what I'd been doing and hope they didn't freak the hell out that I'd done it behind their backs. "I'll get it signed today and sent back."

"Sounds good. Thanks, Easton. And congratulations."

"Thanks." I hung up and read the agreement in detail.

The door to my office opened and I glanced up, expecting Rory.

But it was Gemma leaning against the frame. "So this is where you're hiding?"

I frowned. "Where is your coat?"

"This is my coat." She gestured to the black leather jacket she'd worn to my house. It wasn't thick enough or warm enough for the weather.

"Here." I stood up and took a flannel off the hooks. It would be too big for her, but at least it would add another layer of warmth.

"Is this your way of telling me to get out?" She arched an eyebrow as I handed her the flannel.

"No." My head was still a mess when it came to her and work hadn't helped, but I wouldn't chase her away. She looked too beautiful, her cheeks rosy from the chill outside, and her lips a darker shade of natural pink from my kisses last night.

She came into the office, closing the door behind her and took the chair opposite my desk. "You left without waking me this morning."

"Is that why you're here?"

"Yes." She took a deep breath. "I owe you another apology for last night. I unloaded a lot on you and I'm sorry. I hate that you saw me cry."

This woman. She pretended to have it all together. Except no one did. When would she realize she didn't need to pretend for me?

"It's fine, Gemma."

"It's really not. I apologize for the drama." She folded her hands in her lap, keeping her expression neutral and her posture poised. Her hair was styled, curled in loose waves that fell over her shoulders and down her back. Her eyes were lined with black and shaded with a soft glimmer.

She looked gorgeous this morning. Chic.

Guarded.

Goddamn it. She really was driving me fucking insane. I shook my head, annoyed and frustrated. "Don't. Just . . . stop."

"Stop what?"

"Stop apologizing," I barked. "I don't want a fucking apology."

"Never mind." She held up her hands and stood from the chair, leaving the flannel draped over the arm. "I'll let you get back to work. Clearly, I'm bothering you."

She was two steps out the door when I shot out of my chair and chased her down.

"Oh no, you don't." I gripped her elbow and spun her to face me. "You don't get to run away from me."

"You just snapped at me." She threw an arm toward the office. "I'm not running away. I'm letting you cool off."

"Well, I don't want to cool off. I don't give a damn about the drama. For once, it was nice to see *you*. The real you without all of"—I flung my wrist, motioning up and down her body—"this."

"Clothes? Pretty sure you saw me without all my clothes last night."

"No." I frowned. "With the armor."

"Oh."

"Be real with me." I inched closer, bringing my hands to her shoulders. "If no one else, be real with me."

She dropped her gaze. "I don't know how."

"Yes, you do." I hooked a finger under her chin, tipping it up. "You were last night."

"That was me having a breakdown, then practically begging you to take me to bed. And this morning, I woke up alone. Not that I blame you for sneaking out. If I were you, I wouldn't want to deal with my mess either."

"Now hold up. Me leaving this morning had nothing to do with you crying last night." She'd been all too tempting naked in that bed. The reason I'd left was definitely not because she'd let her guard down.

"Sure," she said, dryly.

"It's the truth. I left this morning because I'm doing my best to keep some distance from you, Gemma."

Another woman might have gotten pissed at me for that comment. But not Gemma. Her eyes softened and the tension in her shoulders fell away. "Can I make another confession?"

I nodded.

"You make me feel things."

"You told me last night. Isn't that what you wanted?"

"Yes," she whispered. "But that doesn't make it any less terrifying."

She had nothing to fear when it came to me. There wasn't a thing she could do that would make me think less of her, make me judge her or make me dislike her.

Except leave again without a goodbye.

"Can I make a confession?"

She nodded. "Yes."

"I'm scared to get too close to you because I know you're eventually going to leave." It was only a matter of time.

"Where does that leave us?" she asked, not denying what we both knew was the inevitable.

I shrugged. "I don't have a damn clue. I wish I could

say I'd steer clear of you and that cabin and we could call this thing quits. But I won't."

"I don't want you to steer clear of me and the cabin, and I don't want to call this quits. What if we kept things casual?"

"Great theory. But you have to know that the minute my mother or my grandmother sees us paired together, casual is out the window."

I wouldn't put it past Grandma to move Gemma into my house, making up some bullshit excuse that the cabin was too cold or too isolated or too small for a single woman in the winter.

"Then let's keep it between us," she said. "Except I already told Katherine."

"She's the only person on this ranch who can keep a secret."

"Then it's settled." Gemma winked, then took a step away. "See you around."

"What?" I tried to catch her but she was already moving backward. "You're leaving?"

"Aren't you working?"

"Yeah." But I didn't want her to go. It was Saturday and instead of sitting behind my desk, I wanted to spend some time with her. "Come with me. I want to show you something."

She gave me a curious glance, but when I turned and marched to the office to get my truck keys, coat and her flannel, she followed.

Gemma played along, not peppering me with questions as I escorted her to my truck. She sat quietly in the passenger seat, her expression relaxed as we drove away from the stables and to the soon-to-be site of the Greer Ranch's latest expansion.

When I pulled over to the edge of the gravel road that ran the length of the new property, she looked around and asked, "What am I looking at?"

"See that right there?" I pointed to the open field out her window and the large barn in the distance. "I just bought it."

"Nice. This is a pretty spot."

Pretty and the setup for the facility was perfect with the flat, wide fields. "My Realtor called me right before you came into the office and told me the buyers accepted my offer. You're the first person I've told."

"Lucky timing on my part."

"No, not just today," I corrected. "At all. I didn't tell anyone I was putting in an offer."

Her eyes widened. "No one?"

"Nope."

The magnitude of what I'd done settled on my shoulders. I'd been so desperate to make a decision without debate or counsel that I'd bought land in secret. My plan was to use the ranch's capital reserves to pay the three-point-one-million-dollar price tag. The money was there and at my discretion. But I should have told my family before making this big a commitment.

Shit. What did that say about my trust in them? Maybe the reason they questioned my decisions and stayed so in the loop was because they feared I'd shut them out.

Which, ironically, I had.

"Was that stupid?" I asked Gemma.

"What will you use it for?"

"I want to expand the horse operation. We're known around the area for our stock. We have some of the best genetics but mostly, we have skill. Cash is one of the best horse trainers around. He's wasted on guest activities."

A smile tugged at her mouth. "So you bought this place for your brother?"

"Partly. And because my gut says it will be a success. Worst case, we use the land for more pasture and expand our cattle operation."

"You did your homework?"

"I did." I had profit and loss projections at my home office and every worst-case scenario plotted out.

"Then no. I don't think this was stupid." She turned to the window again, surveying the frozen ground.

The ice crystals clung to the flaxen grass, reflecting the bright morning sun. The sky stretched powder blue above us, wrapping around the snow-capped mountains rising up around us.

And Gemma seemed to soak it all in. She seemed at ease this morning. She looked comfortable in that seat, wearing my flannel and not minding the smell of dirt and hay that, no matter how many times I cleaned this truck, was permanent.

I'd seen plenty of people come and go from the ranch. It was easy to pick out the guests who'd return on another vacation. Because Montana's rugged and raw landscape called to something deeper in their soul.

They'd found peace here.

It wasn't for everyone but it was in Gemma. How could she not know that she fit here?

Maybe she needed more time. Maybe she needed to see more than the lodge and the cabin.

"What are you doing today?" I asked.

"Nothing much. Why?"

I grinned. "Because I'm going to put you to work."

―――――

"OH, SWEET JESUS, THAT STINKS." Gemma gagged and plugged her nose. "I'm never eating eggs again."

I chuckled and placed another two eggs in the bucket she was carrying. "When I was a kid, Mom's favorite punishment was to make us clean out the chicken coop. I always made sure I was on my best behavior when it had been a couple of months between cleanings."

"I don't think I like chickens." She gave one of the hens perched a sideways glance. "How do I get the eggs from under her butt?"

"Just reach in there and take them."

"You do it."

"Don't be scared. Just brush her aside. She'll move."

"I can't. Please don't make me." Gemma turned her eyes up to me, those hazel orbs melting me into oblivion. How was I supposed to say no to that face?

"Fine." I moved the hen aside, sending her fluttering to the floor and took the eggs.

"Is that it?" Before I had a chance to agree, Gemma ducked out the door.

I shook my head, a smile on my face, and walked out to catch her.

The two of us had spent the morning working together. First, we'd driven to one of the pastures where we'd recently moved a group of about two hundred cows. We drove through, checking on them and looking for any that might be injured. Then we'd circled through an empty meadow that would be next on the rotation, making sure the fence was in good shape.

From there, I'd taken her to one of my favorite places on the ranch—the thousand acres situated directly behind my house.

I'd told her we were checking another section of fence when really, I'd just wanted to spend more time with her peaceful smile as we drove. To listen as she talked to me about nothing. To smell her perfume in my truck.

We'd returned to the lodge to grab a sandwich from the kitchen for lunch and had been halfway through eating when Mom had called to ask if I could gather the eggs from her chickens. She and Grandma had taken a spur-of-the-moment trip to Missoula to spend the day shopping. So Gemma and I had driven to Mom and Dad's place and I'd introduced Gemma to Mom's favorite animals.

"What's next?" Gemma asked after we put the egg basket inside the house where Mom would wash the eggs later.

A warmth spread through my chest that she hadn't asked for me to take her to the Cadillac at the stables. With every job we finished, she was eager for the next. "I was—"

A vehicle door slammed, and I turned away from Gemma, seeing Dad and Granddad climbing out of the truck parked next to mine.

"Hey, guys." Dad waved. "What are you up to?"

"Mom called and asked if we'd gather the eggs. She and Grandma went shopping in Missoula."

"Uh-oh." Dad fished his phone from his pocket and glanced at the screen. "Three missed calls. Guess that means I'd better buzz into the grocery store and have flowers waiting when she gets home."

Mom didn't need flowers. She wasn't the type to get spun up about him not answering his phone. He'd buy her flowers simply because it would make her smile.

"Coffee first." Granddad started up the steps to the front door, his silver travel mug in hand. "I need a refill.

Later on, Easton, we need to talk about calving. Time to get a plan together."

"I have a plan." A detailed plan that outlined staff who'd take the daytime and night rotations to ensure we didn't lose any animals.

"Since when?" He paused on the step. "News to me."

"Me too." Dad nodded.

"Because you're retired. You're both retired." I blew out a long breath and fought to keep my cool. A fight would only ruin the good mood I'd had from a day with Gemma. "I respect you both and your opinions, you know that. I'm grateful that I have a chance to build on your success. Seven years ago, you put me in charge of this ranch. Please, trust me to do my job."

Granddad's face hardened and he opened his mouth, but Dad held up a hand and shot him a look to keep quiet. "You're doing a fine job, son. But it's hard to let go. You'll learn that one day."

"Understandable."

Dad nodded and followed as Granddad continued up the steps.

"Wait," I called. "If you have a minute, there's something I'd like to talk to you both about."

"We've got time. Come on in." Dad motioned me inside as he and Granddad disappeared inside.

"I'll wait in the truck," Gemma said. "Take your time."

"No. You should come in. I want you there when I tell

them about the property." Maybe with her there, they wouldn't disown me. Yet.

"Are you sure? This seems like family business."

She fit into the family, something else I doubted she realized. Besides, it had been her advice to cut them both some slack. And I needed to do a better job of expressing my frustration. I needed to explain in a way they'd hear how I was feeling. Not exactly easy for a guy like me.

Arguing with Dad and Granddad had always been easier than the heart-to-hearts.

"I'm sure. Unless it would make you uncomfortable."

"Not at all." She gave me a reassuring smile and followed me inside. Then she sat at Mom and Dad's kitchen island, pride gleaming in her eyes, as I told my father and grandfather about the land I'd bought and explained my vision for the ranch.

I shocked the hell out of them.

Then they'd shocked the hell out of me.

They'd agreed it was the right opportunity for Cash and that the price for that chunk of land was too good to pass up. By the time we all walked outside—Gemma and me to drive to the stables to get her car while Dad took Granddad home, then went to buy Mom flowers—they were as excited about the expansion as I was.

And tonight, all three of us would tell Cash together.

I opened Gemma's door, holding it for her as she climbed inside, then waved to Dad and reversed my truck out of his driveway.

Gemma pulled her lips together, unsuccessfully hiding a smile as we drove toward the stables.

"Just say it."

She let loose that smile, stealing my breath and the last piece of my heart. "That wasn't so hard, was it?"

CHAPTER TWELVE

EASTON

"Oof," Gemma grunted.

I popped my head out the stall door to see what was happening. She had a bale lifted by the twine and was attempting to heft it toward Sprite's feeder. "Want some help?"

"No." She shot me a warning glare. "I can do this myself."

I held up my hands, chuckling as she shuffled across the floor.

A month ago, she could barely lift the bales an inch. Those square bales were little compared to the ones we used for the cattle. These we kept stocked in the loft for the horses when they weren't out to pasture. They weighed about seventy-five pounds and moving them around by the thin, red baling twine wasn't easy. But she'd been working with me every weekend in the stables and was becoming quite the hand.

Gemma's arms had grown stronger, so had her legs and her core. I knew because I'd seen the definition in her muscles sharpen on the nights I'd spent in her bed at the cabin.

When she had the bale in place, a proud smile stretched across her face as she took the Leatherman I'd lent her this morning from her pocket and cut the twine. Then she went about putting the hay in Sprite's feeder before taking a chunk to Pepsi's empty stall.

I'd let her do the feeding while I'd mucked out a few stalls, a job that I hadn't done in years because I'd hired hands to do it instead. But I'd let Rory go with some of the guys this morning instead of working in the stables. He was out helping prep for the afternoon wagon ride.

Over the past month, he'd spent a lot of Saturdays out with the other staffers. Not only because it gave him more exposure to other tasks, but because it allowed me the chance to work alone with Gemma.

If time with her meant mucking stalls, I'd called it a win.

Thanksgiving was approaching and the resort was at maximum occupancy. Mostly, we catered to hunting parties, but we had some guests who'd come here for a week getaway. We offered wagon rides where they could get a look at the Montana scenery while drinking cocoa or spiked cider. We had families flying in soon who'd stay here through the holiday, enjoying the lodge and the chalets and the renowned chef's food spread.

Meanwhile, my family would all eat together at Grandma and Granddad's place, as was tradition.

And Gemma and I would pretend, like we had been all month, that we were coworkers and friends at best.

If my family had any clue that I drove to Gemma's cabin a few nights a week, no one had mentioned it— which meant they didn't know. Besides my mother, the Greers weren't known for subtlety.

So Gemma and I were keeping up appearances when we crossed paths at the lodge during the week. I didn't stop to talk to her at the front desk. And on Saturdays, when everyone else was at home, this had become our routine. We'd eat Friday night family dinner, limiting conversation and pretending to ignore the other. Then I'd leave first but instead of going home, I'd go to the cabin. By the time Gemma arrived, I'd have a fire roaring and was usually naked in bed, waiting for her to join me. Saturday mornings we'd share a pot of coffee, then I'd come up with a handful of jobs for us to tackle together.

"Okay, I'm done." Gemma appeared at the stall door, brushing her gloves on her jeans.

It was cold outside, the air frozen and the ground covered in a fluffy layer of fresh snow. But there was a light sheen to her brow from working hard and her cheeks were flushed.

She'd shed her navy winter coat—one she'd ordered

weeks ago after I'd lectured her relentlessly for an hour about Montana winters. Over her long-sleeved black tee, she'd shrugged on one of my flannels to keep her clothes from getting too dirty.

Her hair was up in a messy knot because she hadn't washed it this morning when we'd showered together. She wasn't wearing a lick of makeup and a few pieces of straw clung to her boots—another purchase I'd *encouraged* her to make.

Standing there, fresh and relaxed, Gemma stopped my heart. Damn, but she was beautiful.

"Have you ever thought about swapping the storage stall at the end of the stables to one in the middle?" she asked. "It would save foot traffic."

"Um . . . no." That stall at the end of the stables had always been used for storage. I couldn't think of a reason why—that's where it had always been. "But I will."

"Just an idea."

Gemma had been tossing out ideas all month. The way she did it was always more curious than intrusive. But she saw things in a way the rest of us didn't. And so far, I'd taken every single idea she'd pitched.

"What's next?" she asked.

"This." I fisted a handful of her flannel and dragged her into the empty stall, smashing my lips on hers as I pressed her against the wall.

She moaned, her gloved hands sliding up and around my neck as she opened her mouth to let me inside.

My tongue swept against hers and licked in long, smooth strokes. I leaned into her, my cock swelling as she gripped my ass and pulled me closer.

"Easton." My mother's voice resonated in the cavernous space.

I broke away from Gemma instantly, sucking in some air and wiping my lips clean.

Gemma pulled her lips in to hide a smile as she brought one finger to her lips and sunk down against the wall. Hiding.

I was sick of the fucking secrets.

"Easton?"

"Yeah," I called back, scowling at Gemma as I walked out of the stall. "Hey, Mom."

"Hi." She smiled brightly. "How are you today?"

"Fine." I'd been better a second ago. "What's going on?"

"Oh, nothing. I was dropping some extra eggs off at the kitchen and saw your truck, so I wanted to come say good morning."

"Glad you did. Good morning." I held out my elbow so she could loop her arm through mine. Then I walked her down the center aisle. "What are you up to?"

"Not much. I'm—"

"Hello!"

Mom and I turned at Kat's voice, seeing her come inside with a wave.

Since when were the stables such a popular Saturday

spot? Normally, I was the only one who worked on the weekends, besides Katherine. But she usually stayed in the office. Everyone else who'd *retired* worked Monday through Friday.

Mom immediately let my arm go to give Katherine a hug. "Morning, sweetheart."

Katherine kissed Mom's cheek. "I was just on my way to your place but I saw your Jeep. When I went to town yesterday, they had a special on flowers, so I grabbed you a couple of bundles. They're your favorite peach roses."

"Ha." Mom laughed. "Great minds. I went to the store first thing this morning and bought this beautiful pink bouquet I thought you'd like."

As the two of them laughed and talked about flowers, I glanced over to the stall where Gemma was hiding. She could come out. She could pretend to have been working. But she stayed hidden.

"It's been ages since we took a ride together," Mom told Kat. "Let's plan one for this week."

"I'd love to."

"Can you come over for a little while?" Mom asked her, earning a nod as they walked together toward the door.

If I knew them, which I did, they'd spend the rest of the day at Mom's house. She'd lure Kat over with the promise of coffee and cookies, then she'd talk her into staying and helping bake a pie or working on some craft project. It would become a mother-daughter day, Mom having adopted Kat as the daughter she'd always wanted.

I stood and watched until they disappeared outside. "Coast is clear."

Gemma emerged from the stall and her bright smile had dulled. Her eyes went to the door where the sound of Katherine and Mom's slamming vehicle doors echoed. As she stared outside, her expression went blank.

Except I'd spent a month studying Gemma's face. She was doing her best to block out her thoughts and maybe others wouldn't notice, but I saw the hurt she was burying.

"You okay?"

She nodded and forced a smile. "Great."

That was a total lie. But if I pushed, she'd shut me out completely, so I'd wait until she was ready to talk.

"Jigsaw needs a workout. Let's go for a ride."

"Actually, I think I'm going to go—"

"For a ride. With me." I jerked my chin toward Sprite's stall. "Get her curried off. Then I want you to saddle her today."

"What if I don't want to go for a ride?" She fisted her hands on her hips.

"Too bad." I stepped close and took her chin in my grip, holding her gaze for a moment.

There were so many incredible things about this woman. She was smart and driven. She was beautiful and loving. But damn if she wasn't blind.

Would she ever see what was in front of her?

Everything she wanted, everything she needed, was right here. A home. A family.

Me.

I'd stopped lying to myself over the past month. My heart was hers—it had been since the moment she'd nearly knocked me down on the lodge's front porch. I'd stopped pretending that my feelings for her weren't as real as the breath in my lungs or the pulse in my veins.

I'd stopped kidding myself that it wouldn't destroy me when she left.

Because I believed she'd leave.

And I wasn't going to beg her to stay.

"Holler after you get Sprite combed." I leaned in and dropped a kiss on her forehead.

"Okay." She didn't argue because, deep down, I think she needed some air and a ride as much as I did.

It didn't take us long to get the horses ready. Gemma was able to saddle Sprite without much help, remembering most of the steps from our first lesson. I usually only had to show her something once, then she'd tackle it on her own the next time. She remembered the details that most dismissed.

No wonder she'd been so successful in Boston.

The woman was brilliant and her determination to succeed was unmatched.

As we started across the snowy meadow, the horses antsy and happy to be out, Gemma kept her eyes aimed forward. Her coat was bundled up to her neck and she'd pulled on a slouchy beanie.

"Loosen up on the reins," I said. "Sprite's not going to buck you off. Just relax."

Gemma blew out a long breath, doing as I'd instructed.

"Good. Now let's talk. What's wrong, darlin'?"

She didn't say anything for a full two minutes—I counted the seconds tick by—but then she looked at me and shrugged. "I'm jealous."

"Jealous. Of?"

"Katherine. She found a mother. Yours. And I'm so, so happy for her. But I'm jealous too. And I'm angry at myself for being jealous."

She didn't have to be jealous. She could have that same relationship. Gemma had no clue how much love my mother had to give. It was endless. She'd pull Gemma into her life and never let go.

I opened my mouth, unsure what to say, but Gemma spoke first.

"My mother was crazy."

I closed my mouth, watching her profile as she kept her gaze locked on the path ahead. This wasn't the first time she'd hinted at her mother's issues, and unlike her other mentions, I hoped her story wouldn't end here. I hoped she'd keep talking and finally get some of this shit out in the open. To set it free and let the wind carry it away.

"Not like wild and crazy," she clarified. "Crazy, crazy.

It took me a long time after leaving to understand that there was something fundamentally wrong with her. Her mind, it wasn't right."

"What happened? Why'd you run?"

"To stay sane. Things were . . . unlivable. As I got older, it kept deteriorating. Until I knew if I stayed, I'd go mad. I'd end it before I became like her."

The air vanished from my lungs. The pain in my chest was crippling. Gemma was fierce and strong. For her to consider taking her own life . . . things were far worse than I'd ever imagined.

I shifted Jigsaw closer and held out a hand, palm open.

Gemma laid hers on mine and I held it so tight that she'd have to rip it free.

"My mom was beautiful," she said. "I look in the mirror each morning and she's staring right back. I hate that I look like her."

"I'm sorry."

"I almost got a nose job in Boston so I wouldn't be the same. But then I found this great therapist and he helped me see that my looks were my own. Some days though, I still want the plastic surgery. Maybe that's me being weak."

"There's not a damn thing weak about you. I get it." And if she wanted to change her nose or her chin or her cheeks, I'd drive her to the surgeon.

"I want to hate her," Gemma whispered, the words barely audible above the horses' steps and the breeze rolling across the meadow. "It would make everything so much easier, except I don't. I pity her. Her father, my grandfather, raped her from the time she was twelve. It broke her mind."

I gritted my teeth, holding my breath so I wouldn't explode as my temper surged. *Fuck. Fuck. Fuck.* Raped . . . by a parent? It was the unthinkable.

"As you can imagine, she was never right with men." Gemma shook her head. "And thankfully, the bastard had a heart attack when she was six months pregnant with me."

My heart stopped. Gemma had never mentioned her father. Was she—

"No," she answered the question I hadn't been able to think, let alone say aloud. "Once my mom turned eighteen, my grandfather never touched her again. She wasn't interesting enough for him. My father was some guy Mom met at a bar and screwed in a bathroom. She was quite . . . forthcoming about her sexual escapades. She always told me every little detail. Other girls got fairy tales as their bedtime stories. I got detailed comparisons of Mom's lovers."

Gemma truly had lived in a hell.

"Mom worked at a grocery store," she said. "I had a roof over my head and never went hungry. She'd buy me cute clothes from Kmart. I remember her laughing and tickling me when I was little. It's hard for me to pinpoint exactly when I realized she was crazy, and I'd been too young to notice early on. We were poor, but we weren't unhappy. Then everything changed."

"What changed?" I asked.

"Me. I got older. I wasn't as naïve to the boyfriends Mom had always invited to our house. She'd parade me in front of them and say things like, 'Isn't she pretty?' or 'You can touch her hair.'"

My stomach rolled. I wasn't sure I could keep listening to this, but I held her hand and let her talk because this wasn't for me. This was for Gemma. Maybe she'd told a therapist about this, but she needed to air it out here too.

She tightened her grip on my hand. "Most men who came over never came back. They either got what they'd been after from her or they saw Mom's crazy and left."

"Fucking cowards," I spat. "*They* left. But they left you there too."

Hadn't anyone called the cops? Hadn't one of those bastards seen a girl in danger?

"Everything would have been fine if they all would have left," she said. "Some were worse than cowards."

"Gem, did you . . . did they . . ." *Christ.* I couldn't get the words out of my mouth.

"I was never raped. But there are things that happened that I won't ever talk about again."

And I wouldn't put her through reliving that time, especially now when the grip I had on my self-control was slipping. "Okay."

"My mother didn't deserve me."

"That's a damn understatement," I muttered.

"The house that I grew up in was my mother's childhood home. She lived there, even after what my grandfather had done, and after he died."

"That's insane."

"Like I said, she's crazy. And I want to hate her," Gemma repeated. "I very much want to hate her."

I took a few breaths as Gemma stayed quiet, her eyes forward. Jigsaw let out a snort and their footsteps thudded loud against the frozen ground. She tugged her hand free and I let it go, but I stayed close.

Around us, the world seemed so at peace. The snow blanketed everything and the scent of a warm wood fire clung to the air. It seemed so simple. My life seemed so simple. Easy. Blessed.

Gemma was a warrior. She'd fought every day to survive, and I was so proud of her. I was proud that she'd broken the cycle.

"After you ran away, did you ever see her again? Your mother?"

Gemma nodded. "She always knew where I was. I never told anyone, but I went home and checked on her about once a month."

My jaw dropped. "She knew you were living in a junkyard and didn't do anything about it?"

Gemma gave me a sad smile. "She did do something about it. She didn't make me come home."

Maybe there'd been a shred of sanity in her mother after all.

"I don't know what to say."

"There's nothing to say. But now you know. When I see your mother hug Katherine and buy her flowers because she knows how much Katherine loves pink, I get jealous. And Katherine deserves that. She deserves a mother."

"And what about you? Don't you?"

"I have a mother. She lives in the same house she's lived in her entire life. And I bought it five years ago so she doesn't have to work and will never have to move."

"What?" My eyes bulged. "You still . . . you what?"

She'd kept in touch with her mother all these years. She'd provided for her. She'd funded her life.

She wanted to hate her mother. She wanted to change her own looks to escape her mother.

But she'd chained herself to the woman.

God, she was strong. I'd never known anyone with Gemma's strength and resilience.

"I moved out," Gemma said. "I didn't turn my back on her."

"Does Kat know?"

"No one does." There was a warning in her tone.

Gemma had made up her mind about caring for her mother a long, long time ago. And not a soul on earth would make her change her mind, even me.

She tightened her grip on Sprite's reins and clicked

her tongue, picking up the pace and ending the conversation.

I urged Jigsaw forward and caught up, staying silent as I let her choose the path of the ride. Her story ran over and over through my mind, and though I had questions, I kept them to myself.

Where did Gemma and I go from there? Would this confession bring us closer together? Or now that I knew the truth, would it give Gemma the excuse she'd been searching for to run?

Or would she realize that she'd just opened up to me, because she'd finally found the place where she belonged?

CHAPTER THIRTEEN

GEMMA

"Happy Thanksgiving." I smiled into the phone, hearing the baby coo in the background.

"Happy Thanksgiving," Londyn said. "How are you?"

"Cold. It's freezing here. How are things with you?"

"Um . . . interesting."

My smile fell. "Everything okay?"

"I'm pregnant."

"What?" My hand came to my heart. "Really? Congratulations."

"Thanks." Londyn laughed. "This wasn't exactly what we'd planned, but oh my God, Gem, you should see Brooks. He's so excited."

And she was too.

"I'm so happy for you, Lonny."

"Me too. So what are you doing today? Are you eating with the Greers?"

"I'm sitting outside Carol and Jake's house as we speak."

"How's the Cadillac fairing in the snow?" she asked.

"Not too bad. Though I think it'll be happy to see warm weather again." Easton had offered to get me a ranch truck to drive around, but I'd declined. For now, the Cadillac was doing fine on the roads they kept plowed. And if that changed, I'd take a truck.

"Are you still thinking you'll leave after Christmas?"

"Unless the roads are bad." The idea of leaving made my heart ache, but eventually, my time here would come to an end.

It had to end.

Dreams were only meant to last a few short hours. Already I'd had mine for weeks.

"There's no rush," Londyn said for the hundredth time since I'd left West Virginia. Every time we'd talked, she'd reminded me to take some time.

"I know, but this entire stay in Montana was just a vacation," I lied. "It's time to move on."

To where, I wasn't sure. After I delivered the Cadillac to Karson, I had no idea where to go next. But I had twelve hundred miles to figure it out.

A wail sounded in the background. "Uh-oh."

"She's exhausted." Londyn sighed. "Too much excitement today and she's fighting sleep."

"I'll let you go. Bye." I hung up the phone but didn't get out of the car.

Mine was the only one in the driveway besides Liddy's Jeep and even though Easton wasn't inside, I wanted a moment to prepare for tonight.

Things between us had been different over the past two weeks—uncomfortable and distant—and it had everything to do with my past.

I should have stayed quiet on that horseback ride. I shouldn't have told him about my mother.

Easton came over a few times a week and we'd have dinner together. We'd have sex. But there was a distance between us, even when we'd fall asleep in the same bed. I found his gaze waiting for me more often than not, and in the quiet moments, he'd look at me like he was expecting me to decide something.

Except what was there to decide? I wasn't going to cut off my mother. No matter how much I struggled with her as a parent and what she'd done to me, she had no one in the world except me. If he wanted me to disown her, he'd be disappointed.

What the hell had I been thinking telling him everything? Why couldn't I have just kept my mouth shut?

And now I had to survive another family function as the one non-family member. I'd pretend that everything was fine. I'd pretend to be happy.

And I'd pretend not to be in love with Easton.

The days were getting harder and harder to endure. Every hour I had to remind myself this was temporary.

And the longer I stayed, the more painful it would be to drive away.

Easton hadn't asked me to stay. He *wouldn't* ask me to stay. This was casual. This was for fun. He certainly hadn't insisted we stop hiding our relationship from his family.

But what if we did? What if we told them we were together? What if I came back after driving the Cadillac to California?

Would he want me back?

"Are you coming inside?" Carol hollered from the front door.

I nodded and pushed open the door to the Cadillac, stepping outside and hurrying to the door. The snow was falling lightly and I brushed the stray flakes from my shoulders and my hair before stepping inside. "Happy Thanksgiving."

"You too." Carol took the gift bag from my hand, peeking inside, as I shrugged off my coat. "Oh, you are so sweet. These are gorgeous. Thank you."

"You're welcome." I smiled as she slid out the charcuterie board I'd found at a gift shop in Missoula last weekend. I'd skipped the last two Saturdays with Easton, using holiday shopping as an excuse for two trips into Missoula.

Leaving the ranch had been good for me. It had been a reminder that there was an entire world out there for me to explore, and with my disposable income, I could go anywhere I wanted. There was more to the world than the Greer Ranch.

A month ago, that idea had excited me. Now, it made my stomach knot.

"Are you okay?" Carol asked. "You seem distracted."

"No, I'm great," I lied. "Can I help with anything?"

"Of course not. You're our guest, so you can sit down and relax."

Right. I was the guest.

The kitchen island was loaded with appetizers. There was a spinach dip and a wheel of brie. Crackers. Olives. Prawns. Three bottles of wine were open and four different bottles of whiskey were out beside a handful of tumblers.

The smell of a cooking turkey filled the air and Liddy was at the sink, peeling potatoes. "Hey, Gem."

"Hi." I loved that she called me Gem. There weren't many who did, just those I loved. "This looks amazing."

"Help yourself." Carol handed me a glass of wine. "I hope you haven't eaten anything all day. We'll never get through all this."

The doorbell rang as she popped an olive into her mouth.

"I'll get it." Before she could argue and remind me again that I was a guest, I set down my wine and hurried to the door, expecting Katherine. Besides me, she was the only one who rang the doorbell. But it wasn't my friend standing on the stoop.

It was the bartender from town. Liz—*funny* Liz.

"Hey there." She smiled, taking a step forward to cross the threshold.

"H-hi." I shook out of my stupor and moved aside, holding the door for her. Then I remembered my manners. "I'm Gemma."

She hung up her coat as I closed the door, then held out a hand. "Liz. Nice to officially meet you."

"You too." Normally, I'd make polite conversation, but my mind went blank.

Liz wore a fitted sweater dress. It was far from scandalous with its long sleeves and turtleneck, but paired with her knee-high boots, she looked beautiful and sexy. Her hair was pinned up in a pretty knot and her makeup was elegant.

I was in black jeans and a plain sweater that was far from sexy. I hadn't even worn heels.

"Liz, welcome." Carol breezed past me and pulled Liz into a hug. "What are you drinking tonight?"

"Wine, please. Thanks for having me."

"You're always welcome. I'm just glad JR ran into you at the store yesterday."

"Me too." Liz laughed. "This is much better than a chicken pot pie at home alone."

So she was here, a guest like me, who would have been alone for Thanksgiving if the Greers hadn't come to her rescue.

The door behind us opened, forcing us all deeper

inside as Cash walked in with Katherine following close behind.

Hugs and greetings were exchanged as Jake and JR came in from the den where they'd been playing pool. Each carried a tumbler of whiskey in their hand.

Unless there were more guests, everyone was here except Easton. The others had barely removed their coats when the door opened and he stepped inside.

His eyes found mine immediately and hope bloomed that he'd be different tonight. But then his eyes flickered straight to Liz and a broad smile stretched across his handsome face. "Hey, Liz. Glad you could make it."

Wait, he'd known she was coming? And he hadn't mentioned it to me?

Nice.

The group shuffled toward the kitchen, everyone collecting drinks and sampling the pre-dinner smorgasbord. I stuck close to Katherine, not wasting any time as I drained my first glass of wine.

Easton was kind enough to pour Liz's glass.

I refilled my own.

"Did your parents make it to Texas?" JR asked Liz.

"They did. And they've already inundated my phone with photos of the baby." She took out her phone and pulled up one of the photos, earning a sigh from Katherine and Liddy as they took in the pink bundle.

"That's my new niece," Liz told me. "My brother lives in Austin and he and his wife just had a baby on

Monday. My parents flew down to spend the week with them."

Leaving her here alone for Thanksgiving.

"She's beautiful," I said, honestly. There was something about a baby's pout that always melted my heart.

I wasn't sure if I'd get to be a mother. At the rate I was going, it was unlikely, but I'd be a good aunt. Londyn's daughter, Ellie, would be loved beyond measure.

"I wanted to go"—Liz set her phone aside—"but someone had to be around to run the bar."

"Liz's family has owned the Clear River Bar for, what?" JR asked her. "Thirty years?"

She nodded. "Started by my grandfather."

"He and I went to school together," Jake added. "A hell of a long time ago."

"Remember that time your granddad came out here and tried to steal my horse?" JR chuckled. "Swore up and down that I'd been so drunk at the poker table the night before that I'd forgotten I'd bet my horse and he'd won."

She giggled. "He was such a goof."

An hour later, I'd lost count of the number of stories the group had told about Liz's family or tales from her bar. She fit into the mix so well, that with each one, my status as guest felt more and more obvious.

Liz had been Cash's date to their senior prom. Liz had thrown Katherine's twenty-first birthday party. Liz had gone skiing with Easton a few years ago and had come home with a broken nose, courtesy of a tree branch.

Liz. Liz. Liz.

She was sweet. She was funny and charming.

And she was infatuated with the man who'd been sharing my bed.

The way she smiled at him was subtle, like a girl who'd learned to hide her long-time crush well. Unless you were looking closely—which I was—it might seem like a tight friendship. But her eyes were on him a tad too often. When he laughed, her cheeks flushed. She made to stand beside him, casually shifting whenever he moved.

And the part I hated most was that he'd be better off with someone like her.

By the time we sat at the dining room table, I'd lost my appetite. The three glasses of wine I'd consumed had given me a sharp headache.

Easton held out Liz's chair, taking the seat beside her, per Carol's seating assignments.

I was ushered to the chair directly across from them, giving me the perfect seat to watch the two reminisce.

But he didn't look at me, not once. Easton was keeping up his end of the bargain, pretending like I was nothing more than the fleeting guest.

Even if we weren't pretending, what could I contribute to this trip down memory lane? I couldn't razz him about the time in college when he'd brought his girlfriend, the vegetarian, home to a cattle ranch only to have her dump him one week later. I didn't know the name of his dog that had died in eighth grade or the truck he'd driven in high school.

I didn't know much about Easton's past because he'd never offered much up.

No, I was the headcase we normally examined. I had to give him credit. Easton listened like he cared, but really, I doubted he'd wanted to know the horrid details.

It hadn't stopped me from blathering on though, had it? God, I was so stupid.

I didn't fit here. These were nice people, but even Katherine fit in better. She knew where to get the silverware from Carol's kitchen to help set the table. She knew where the dishes went after unloading the dishwasher. She offered to fix Jake and JR a drink and knew without asking how they took their whiskey.

"You okay?" Katherine whispered at my side as we passed platters and bowls of the feast around.

"Yeah," I lied. "Just a bit of a headache."

Katherine knew Easton and I were sleeping together, but whenever we'd talked, I'd downplayed my feelings for him. She thought we were casual. She thought we were fleeting. She didn't know how much I'd grown to care for him and she definitely didn't know I'd had a jealous breakdown about Liz.

"Do you want me to get you some Advil?" She pointed toward the bathroom down the hall because she knew where they kept the medicine. That shouldn't have annoyed me, but it did.

"I'll be fine." I scooped a heaping spoonful of stuffing on my plate. "Nothing some carbs and more wine won't knock out."

"Amen." She picked up her fork and dug into her candied yams.

With any luck, we'd all be too busy eating for much more conversation. And once this meal was over, I'd explain my headache was unbearable and return to the cabin where I'd barricade myself in the bedroom, hide under the covers and *if* Easton showed up, he'd find the door locked.

"So, Gemma. You and Katherine grew up together, right?" Liz asked.

"That's right." I looked to Katherine who gave me a slight headshake, which meant she'd told the Greers about our childhood, but not the local bartender.

I doubted many others outside this family knew how we'd grown up because it wasn't easy to share.

"And you're working at the lodge?" Liz asked.

I nodded. "Just while I'm here. Katherine was nice enough to give me something to do until Christmas."

"Oh, I didn't realize you were leaving. I thought you lived here."

"No, she doesn't." Easton spoke before I could answer. He finally dared to make eye contact.

Those eyes were unreadable. The tone of his voice wasn't flat or annoyed or cold, it was just matter-of-fact.

I didn't live here.

So why stay until Christmas? This dare, his challenge, didn't matter. I had nothing to prove, not anymore.

I'd already lost.

"I'm on my way to California," I told Liz. "I just came to visit Katherine."

"Ah." She nodded and there was no mistaking the hint of relief in her gaze. She'd pegged me as competition, even though Easton excelled at making sure I looked insignificant to him. Liz nudged Easton's elbow with her own. "I'm going snowmobiling next weekend. Want to come?"

"Maybe. What day?"

"Saturday. Mom and Dad will be back to cover the bar."

I held my breath, waiting to hear his answer. Saturdays were our day. Or at least they had been until I'd opened my mouth and told him about Mom.

"Let me see how the week shakes out," he told her. "Maybe."

Maybe.

He hadn't said no.

My nose stung with the threat of tears but I kept them at bay, taking a long drink of my wine and concentrating on the meal.

Conversation around me continued, light and jovial and festive. But the delicious food had lost its flavor. The wine wasn't numbing the pain. And the headache I'd lied to Katherine about began pounding in my temples.

It was only by sheer force and years of practice that

I managed to hold a slight smile through dinner. But when Jake mentioned giving it an hour before eating dessert, I knew my façade wouldn't survive the rest of the night.

"Excuse me." I stood from the table and went to the powder room, closing my eyes once the door was locked and dragging in a shaky breath.

I just wanted to go home.

But where was home? Boston? California? The cabin?

None of those places were home. I was filthy rich and utterly homeless. The closest thing I had was that Cadillac outside.

Maybe it was time to get in it and get on with my life.

I washed my hands and gave myself a few minutes to compose my emotions, then I returned to the main room, finding Carol and Liddy in the kitchen clearing plates. "Thank you both for an incredible meal."

"You're welcome." Liddy smiled. "Would you like more wine?"

"Actually, I think I'm going to get going. I'm getting a nasty headache and I don't want to infect everyone with a lousy mood."

"Oh, no." Carol rushed around the island for a hug. "Do you want to rest in the guest bedroom and see if it passes?"

"My sweatpants are calling. I think I'll just sneak out."

"You go on ahead. We understand."

Liddy came over and hugged me goodbye, then

without returning to the dining room, I gathered my coat from the hook beside the door and slipped into the night.

The Cadillac's tires crunched on the hard snow as I steered the car on the bumpy road to the cabin. It was quiet outside, not a breath of wind rustled through the trees. The black and soundless night only made it more obvious I was alone.

That there was only one heartbeat in the car. There were only one set of footsteps in the fresh snow outside the cabin. There was only one jacket to hang on the coat hook.

Easton's scent clung to the air and I could smell his spice. I dragged in a deep breath, wanting so much to curl into a ball on the couch and cry.

It wasn't his fault. Easton was being nice to his friend and nothing he'd done tonight had been remotely flirtatious. Like a typical man, Easton probably didn't even know Liz had feelings for him.

This urge to scream and wail was not on him. This was my issue.

Yet another to add to my growing collection.

Tears welled in my eyes, but I swiped them away and marched to the bedroom.

I knew when it was time to leave. I'd had this same feeling at sixteen. I'd had this same feeling in Boston.

My time here was over. Montana wasn't the place for me anymore.

So I dragged my empty suitcase from the closet.

And packed.

CHAPTER FOURTEEN

EASTON

"Here, I'll take that." I stood from the table, collecting Liz's empty plate to take to the kitchen along with my own.

"Oh, I can help." She began to stand but I shook my head.

"Nah. You sit. I've got it." Something was wrong with Gemma and I'd been looking for a reason to leave the dining room, but I hadn't wanted to make it obvious.

Mom and Grandma were in the kitchen and I'd expected to find Gemma with them, but she was nowhere in sight. "Here you go."

"Thanks." Grandma took the dishes from my hand and put them in the sink. "I'm going to grab the ice cream from the freezer in the garage, Liddy. Just in case anyone wants dessert."

"Okay." Mom pushed the start button on the dishwasher. "I'll get out the pies."

As she buzzed around the kitchen, I walked into the living room, thinking Gemma had wanted a quiet moment alone, but the room was empty. Where was she?

"She's not here."

I turned around at Mom's voice. "Who?"

"Gemma." She rolled her eyes. "You two might be fooling everyone else, but I wasn't born yesterday."

"Oh," I muttered.

I shouldn't have been surprised. Mom had a nose for secrets.

Cash and I had only gotten away with throwing one bonfire kegger at the ranch. She'd sniffed out all the other planning attempts and had smothered them. And she'd admitted years ago that the only reason we hadn't been busted for the one successful party was because I'd been in college and it had been Cash's senior year sendoff.

"Where'd she go?" I asked.

"She wasn't feeling well."

"What?" My gaze whipped to the window, and sure enough, the Cadillac was gone. "She's sick?"

Gemma had been fine this morning when I'd left the cabin. I hadn't seen her at the lodge today, but when I'd arrived here tonight, she'd appeared okay. Not that I'd outright asked her because when we were here, I didn't talk to her. I did my best to treat her like an acquaintance. I didn't want anyone to notice the way I looked at her, so

I'd decided it was better not to glance at her in the first place.

"She said she had a headache," Mom said.

"Since when?"

"I'm guessing since Liz arrived." Mom shook her head, glancing over her shoulder to make sure we were alone. "I love your father, but that man can be thick as a brick wall sometimes."

"Huh?"

Mom pursed her lips. "Like father like son."

"What did I do?" I scowled.

She reached up and flicked the shell of my ear.

"Ouch." My hand flew to rub the sting. Mom hadn't flicked my ear like that since I'd been a teenager. "Seriously?"

"Shame on you, Easton Greer. If that girl stays after the way you treated her, I'll be shocked."

"What should I have done, Mom?" I stepped closer, careful to keep my voice low. "Gemma and I agreed to keep this between us. We don't need anyone else involved when she's just going to leave in a few weeks. And I couldn't exactly ignore Liz. Dad invited her, not me. But I don't blame him. She would have been alone at Thanksgiving."

"I know." She sighed. "Don't get me wrong. I like Liz. I actually thought Cash would chase after her one of these days."

"Really?"

"Yeah. Not that he'd have any luck. She's always had a crush on you." She cast her eyes to the ceiling. "My boys are both clueless."

"I'm not—wait, what? Liz doesn't have a crush on me."

Mom flicked my ear again.

"Jesus Chr—"

"Language." She pointed a finger at my nose.

"Sorry." I rubbed my ear again. "What was that for?"

"That was for Gemma. Because you were so busy not looking at her, you missed the way Liz *was*. That's why Gemma left, fighting tears and faking a headache, because you are so worried she's going to leave that you're practically pushing her out the door."

"Because she *is* leaving. Why drag all of you into this? Why get everyone's hopes up that she's going to stay when she won't?"

After hearing Gemma's story about her mother, I didn't blame her for leaving. She deserved to find the place she wanted to stay. She deserved the life of her choosing. She'd been forced into too much.

So I wouldn't beg her to stay for me. I wouldn't guilt her into a life here simply because it would make my dreams come true.

I was in love with Gemma.

I loved her enough to set her free. This was her decision to make.

"She wants a home, son."

"I know."

Mom put her hand to my cheek. "Then give her one."

If only it were that easy.

"Oh, sorry." Behind Mom, Liz stopped at the edge of the room. "I didn't mean to interrupt."

"It's fine." There wasn't much more I could explain to Mom without delving into Gemma's past. And that was her story to tell, not mine.

"Should we have dessert?" Mom gave me a tight smile, then turned and walked for the kitchen.

"Actually, I'm going to take off."

She glanced over her shoulder and nodded, knowing exactly where I was headed. "See you tomorrow."

"Happy Thanksgiving, Mom. Thanks for cooking."

"My pleasure." Mom's expression was a mix of hope and worry—though not for me. Mom loved Gemma too. And she was counting on me to make this right.

But what if the only way to make it right was to let Gemma drive away?

She'd break my heart but I'd stand back and watch her go.

It would hurt us both far more if I had to watch her fade away simply because I'd asked her to live the life *I* wanted.

"You're leaving already?" Liz asked, following me to the door.

"Yeah." I took my coat off the hook and shrugged it on. "It's been a long day and there's always work tomorrow."

"It was nice to see you."

"You too. I'll stop by the bar one of these nights and beat you at a game of dice."

"Ha." She huffed. "You wish. When was the last time you beat me? Six? Seven years ago?"

I chuckled. "To be fair, you get more time to practice."

"True." She smiled. "Are you just going home?"

Eventually. But first, I had to make a stop at the cabin. "Yep," I lied and zipped up my coat.

Liz stepped close, too close, and traced her finger up my arm. "Want some company?"

Well, shit.

"Look, Liz, I—"

"Don't say it." She cringed and stepped away, slapping a hand to her forehead. "I'm sorry. We're friends. I shouldn't have done that. I'm stupid."

"You're not stupid. I just don't feel that way about you."

She met my gaze, her own screaming *why?*

"I'm with someone."

Her forehead furrowed, then her eyes went to the door and the space where Gemma's Cadillac had been parked. "Oh, it's Gemma, isn't it?"

"Yeah."

"Can we forget this happened? Please?" she pleaded.

I nodded. "Sure."

"Thanks, Easton." She took another step away. "See you around."

"See ya, Liz." We both knew I wouldn't be in to play

dice. Even if Gemma wasn't in the picture, even if Gemma hadn't captured my heart, Liz would only ever be a friend. I wouldn't lead her on. Hell, maybe I'd been leading her on.

Once again, Mom was right.

When it came to women, I was thick as a brick wall. Someday, I'd remember that my mother was always right.

I slipped outside without saying goodbye to the others. Tomorrow, I'd run into town and get Mom and Grandma flowers for all their work, but tonight, my gut was yelling that something was wrong with Gemma and it wasn't a headache.

The cabin's lights were on and a stream of smoke trailed from the chimney. I didn't bother knocking at the door and let myself inside. "Gem?"

A drawer slammed in the bedroom before she emerged in the hallway. Her hair was up in a ponytail and her face was flushed. "So you just let yourself in?"

"So you just left without a word?"

"I didn't realize we were speaking when other people were around." She fisted her hands on her hips. "My bad."

"I didn't come here to fight." I paused in the middle of unzipping my coat. "Do you want me to go?"

For a second, I thought she'd say yes. But then the angry look on her face softened and she pinched the bridge of her nose. "No."

"Are you feeling all right? Mom said you were sick."

"I'm fine," she muttered and walked my way as I hung up my coat. "Want something to drink?"

"No, I'm good."

She passed me on her way to the kitchen, not looking at me directly, so I slipped off my boots and followed, standing behind her as she took out a glass and filled it with some water from the tap.

"Hey." I stepped into the space behind her, lifting the glass from her hand and setting it beside the sink. "There's nothing with Liz."

"I know. You're friends."

"Yes. We're friends. I've known her a long time. But that's where it ends. And after you left, I made sure she understood that."

"It's fine." She waved it off and tried to move away, but I wrapped my arm around her shoulders and pulled her back against my chest.

"What's wrong?"

Gemma hung her head. "Nothing."

"Try again."

"I don't fit here, Easton," she whispered, and my heart cracked.

Maybe I'd seen this coming. Maybe I should have expected it sooner. But these past two weeks as Gemma had pulled away, I should have seen it as the beginning of a goodbye.

I let her go and took a step away.

She turned to face me. "I'm not what you need."

I scoffed. "Spare me that, okay? You walk away from here, that's your choice. But don't play the martyr."

"I'm not playing at anything. It's the truth."

"You made the decision for me. Why? Because Liz was at dinner?"

"It's not about her."

"Bullshit."

She shot me a glare, then stormed out of the kitchen for the bedroom.

My temper spiked as she disappeared down the hallway and I marched after her.

"Why—" My question fell away as I reached the doorway. There was an open suitcase on the bed with most of Gemma's clothes inside. "You're leaving."

"I'm leaving." She yanked the nightstand drawer open and took out the few things she'd stashed inside. A lip balm and a box of condoms got thrown on the suitcase pile.

It was impossible to take a full breath. My chest felt tight like someone had wrapped it in steel.

I was supposed to have until Christmas. I was supposed to have time to prepare for this.

I wasn't ready.

"Would you have even said goodbye?" I asked.

She stood from the drawer, throwing a hand lotion onto the bed, and her shoulders drooped. "No."

It was eleven years ago all over again.

Well, fuck that. I wasn't letting her slip out again. This

time, she could watch me walk away when I was goddamn ready to leave.

I blew into the room, my rage a force, and took her face in my hands. I held it tight, then slammed my mouth on hers in a hard, brutal kiss.

Gemma melted against me, surrendered, as I poured my frustration into her lips. She leaned into it, taking everything I had. She let me punish her with this kiss.

Except I didn't want to punish her. I wanted to love her and keep her and . . . *fuck*. It would break her.

I tore my mouth away and dragged in a jagged breath as I dropped my forehead to hers. Her scent was everywhere, and I realized how foolish I'd been not to take her to my bed. Because I had nothing of hers to keep. When she left this cabin, she'd be gone.

"I'm sorry." Her voice cracked. "I don't—"

"It's okay." I cupped her cheek and leaned away to meet her eyes. They were full of unshed tears. When one dripped down the smooth curve of her cheek, I wiped it away with my thumb. "It's okay."

She stood on her toes, brushing her lips against mine. This time, it was my turn to melt. I wrapped her up tight, holding her close as she opened her mouth to let my tongue sweep inside.

I'd memorize her taste. I'd memorize the way she felt in my arms. I'd do all of that because I hadn't all those years ago.

This time around, I wouldn't lose her memory so quickly.

Our hands fumbled to strip clothing as we shuffled to the bed. Her sweater came first so I could mold my hands over the black satin of her bra. Her nipples pebbled beneath the fabric, digging into the flesh of my palm. My button-up came next, followed by the white T-shirt underneath.

When the backs of her knees hit the edge of the mattress, I eased her down and flicked the button open on her jeans so I could drag them off her legs. With them gone, the only thing left on the bed was Gemma in her bra and panties. And that fucking suitcase.

I shoved it to the floor.

Gemma scowled as her clothes spilled everywhere.

I shrugged and unbuckled my belt. If this was the last time, I wasn't going to be hindered by that fucking luggage.

Gemma sat up and ran her hands across my stomach, her pink nails digging into the dips between each muscle. Then she ripped the button free and tugged down the zipper. The moment I sprang free, her tongue was on me, licking the tip of my cock before taking me completely into her mouth.

"Gem." I cupped the back of her head. "Fuck."

She moaned and the vibration of her throat nearly tipped me over the edge.

I pulled her off me with her ponytail, then I shoved off

my jeans, and tore at her panties while she unclasped her bra. When I covered her naked body with my own, she wound her legs around my hips. Our eyes locked. Our breaths mingled. And when I slid inside her bare, I wrapped her in my arms so she'd feel the beat of my heart.

It was hers.

And when she left here tomorrow, she'd take it on the road.

Gemma trembled beneath me, her legs cinching tighter to pull me deeper.

"I need to get a condom," I whispered in her ear.

She shook her head, her arms holding me close. "Not yet."

I loved this woman. Damn, did I love her. But if I didn't put a condom on now, there'd be no chance I'd stop again. And as much as I wanted to see her growing with our child, that would only make things worse.

So I pulled free as a groan of protest escaped her lips and riffled around the floor until I found the box of condoms. When I rejoined her on the bed, she spread her legs wide and welcomed me home.

"You feel so good." I kissed her open mouth. "So fucking good."

She hummed her agreement against my lips as I rocked us together, taking her higher, stroke after stroke. When her legs began to tremble and her breath hitched, I reached between us and found her clit.

One touch and she detonated. She pulsed around me

with wave after wave of pleasure, causing her body to quake. The squeeze of her inner walls and the sheer ecstasy on her face was too much. Tingles raced down my spine and my blinding orgasm broke.

We held tight to one another, grasping for just one more second together. Our bodies were slick with sweat and her ear was against my lips. The words I wanted to whisper begged to be free. *I love you.* I wanted to say them. I wanted her to know that she meant everything to me. But I swallowed them down because I wouldn't make her deny them or repeat them. I wouldn't give her anything to feel guilty about when she left.

Before I eased away and stood from the bed, I kissed the underside of her jaw, then her collarbone, stealing little tastes while I could. Then I left her on the bed while I went to the bathroom to deal with the condom.

Maybe tonight, if I could talk to her and get her to relax, I could find out where her head was at. I could find out what had happened and see if I could delay this for a couple more weeks. If I got really lucky, we'd get five feet of snow and she'd be stuck here until spring.

It might only delay the inevitable, but it might be my only chance to give her the time to change her mind. To decide on this ranch as a home.

On me.

I washed up and expected to find her in bed when I got back to the room. Instead, she was dressed. Her hair was twisted in a messy knot and she was on her knees beside the suitcase.

She wasn't putting the clothes back in the dresser.

She was packing them to leave.

So much for one last night.

I swiped my jeans off the floor and jerked them on, leaving the belt hanging loose. Gemma held out my T-shirt and I ripped it from her hands before pulling it over my head. I couldn't see my button-up in the mess, but I wasn't going to stick around and search for it.

"When?" I barked.

"When what?" Her voice was calm and quiet.

"When are you leaving?"

"Tomorrow, I guess."

I scoffed and searched the mess on the floor for my socks. When I found them, I shoved them in my pocket and spun for the door without a word.

If she wasn't staying, neither was I. Sleeping beside her for another night, having her curled into my side, would be torture.

I stalked to the door, taking my coat from the hook and not bothering to put it on while I stepped into my boots. My anger would be enough to keep me warm all the way home.

Gemma's footsteps stomped on the floor as she came down the hallway. "So that's it? You come here, fuck me and leave?"

"Are you kidding me? Fuck, you drive me insane." I

raked a hand through my hair. "You're the one who's hell-bent on racing out of here in the morning. What do you want from me?"

"You? What about me? What do you want from me?"

I want you to stay. More than anything, I wanted her to stay.

But I wasn't going to beg. If she chose this life, if she chose me, she'd have to be sure. Because the minute she said yes, I'd hold on and never let go.

I wanted her to make her own choice.

"I'm not going to beg you to stay, Gemma."

Something flashed in her eyes, but before I could make sense of it, she blinked it away. Then she reached past me to whip the door open, and with one hand pressed into my chest, she shoved me outside.

Right before she slammed the door in my face, I heard her whisper, "No one ever does."

CHAPTER FIFTEEN

GEMMA

"What else is happening?" I asked Benjamin. "That's it," he said. "Everything is under control."

"Okay. Good."

I'd called him to check in, like I did every Friday morning. And per usual, there wasn't much to report. Since I'd left Boston, Benjamin had done exactly what I'd asked. He'd taken over.

Each week, he had fewer questions for me to answer. Fewer tasks for me to complete. It should have made me feel good that I'd put such a competent and capable man in charge. Benjamin was caring for my investments and capital ventures like they were his own.

But I'd come to dread these Friday morning phone calls because they were another blunt reminder that I wasn't really needed.

Not in Boston.

And not in Montana.

I'd leave the Greer Ranch today and though Annabeth would be disappointed that once again the front-desk position would be vacant, she'd eventually find my substitute. Katherine had other friends to hang out with. And Easton . . .

For the moment, I wasn't ready to process the heartache of leaving Easton Greer. Of knowing he'd eventually find a better replacement. So I wouldn't think about Easton, not today. I'd save that for my road trip.

"How are things in Montana?" Benjamin asked.

"Coming to an end. I'm leaving today."

"O-oh. Really? I thought you were staying until Christmas."

"Change of plan." My stomach twisted. It had been in a constant knotted state since Easton had left last night.

I'd done my best to fight back tears, mostly by throwing myself into packing. Then I'd cleaned the cabin, tongue-and-groove ceiling to hardwood floor. Finally, I'd fallen asleep from sheer exhaustion—emotional and physical—and had woken up with the sunshine streaming through the cabin's bedroom window.

It hadn't taken me long to load up the Cadillac, though there was more in the trunk now than when I'd started this journey. I had the winter coat Easton had insisted upon along with the boots I'd used on our working Saturdays.

And I had the plaid shirt he'd left behind last night, tucked safely inside my purse.

All that remained was to finish this call, stop by and say goodbye to Katherine, then get on the highway.

"Would you mind booking me a hotel room?" I asked.

"When and where?"

"I'll find some motel along the road tonight, but I was hoping to get to San Francisco tomorrow and stay there for a few days." I needed to build up some mental walls before venturing to Temecula. I wasn't sure if I had the strength to stop by and visit my mother, but it was something I'd been considering.

"The usual amenities?" he asked, the sound of computer keys clicking in the background. He'd probably already pulled up a travel website.

"Please." Benjamin knew I'd prefer a boutique hotel with a spa and five-star menu.

"Done. I'll email you the details. Anything else?"

"No, thank you. I'll check in later. Have a good week."

"Gemma, wait. Before you hang up."

My heart stopped. *Please, please don't quit.* I couldn't handle it right now. I couldn't deal with leaving the Greer Ranch and having Benjamin leave me all in the same day. "Yeah?"

"Are you okay?" There was genuine concern in his voice, probably because mine sounded flat and lifeless.

"Sure. I'm great."

There was a long pause on the other end of the line.

No doubt he was debating whether or not it would be smart to call his boss on a blatant lie. Thankfully, he let it go. "Would you like company in San Francisco?"

"Who? *You?*"

"Yes, *me*. I've missed you."

"I've missed you too." My eyes flooded.

As much as I would like to see a familiar face, my days in San Francisco would be miserable. I had a broken heart to mend. It would be better to see Benjamin when the two of us could laugh and talk without a cloud of sorrow hanging over my head.

"How about we meet up after I deliver this Cadillac? We can spend a week or two somewhere tropical. Bring Taylor and the three of us will spend a small fortune gorging ourselves on food between spa appointments. You two can pick where we go."

He chuckled. "Taylor is going to want Bali."

Escaping to the opposite end of the world with Benjamin and his spouse seemed like a good idea at the moment. "Bali it is."

"Keep in touch, please. I don't like the idea of you driving alone."

"I'll be fine," I assured him. "Talk soon."

"Bye."

With the call over, I tucked my phone into my purse and slung it over my shoulder. Then I stood from the couch in the living room and took one last look at the cabin.

My temporary home.

It had always felt temporary. That had to mean something, right? That I'd never wanted to live here forever? I liked the cabin. It was cozy and warm. But it wasn't home.

This place wasn't home.

So I drew in another breath, savoring one last inhale of the fire I'd built this morning that had nearly burned out. Then I walked to the door, twisted the lock on the handle before closing it behind me and got in the car.

I wouldn't let myself look in my mirror as I drove away.

It was simply another fleeting stop.

And like I'd done before, it was time to search for the next.

───────

"STAY ANOTHER WEEK," Katherine pleaded. "Or two."

"I can't."

"Please? I already have your Christmas present. Just stay until then."

She wasn't making this easy on me. Our friendship had bloomed in my time here and I'd miss her terribly. I dearly hoped our relationship wouldn't end.

"I'm going to miss you." I pulled her into a hug and squeezed tight.

We were standing in the middle of her office. I'd found

her behind her desk, as always, working with a smile on her face.

I envied that and so much else. But I was so happy for her. I was glad she'd found her place.

"Call me," I said. "And I'll call you. I don't want to lose you again."

"You won't." Her arms cinched tighter. "What happened, Gemma? Why are you leaving? You seemed happy."

I was happy.

But I wasn't going to mix up Easton's life. Especially if he wasn't going to ask me to stay.

Last night, I'd felt sixteen again. When I'd left my mother's home, she'd been there. Watching. She'd sat on the living room couch and watched me walk out the door without a word.

I'd cried for ten blocks knowing she wouldn't chase after me.

That pain had been nothing compared to Easton's declaration he wouldn't beg me to stay.

But I wasn't thinking about that. Not now.

My priority was to get on the road and drive.

One of these days, maybe I wouldn't feel so lost. Maybe one day I'd set foot into the place where I was meant to be and know, in my bones, it was mine. Maybe I'd finally quiet the unsettled energy that zipped through my veins.

"I have to go." I let Katherine go and blinked away the threat of tears. "You have my number."

She nodded, swiping at her own eyes. "Are you going to come back?"

"Someday." Maybe.

But only when I could handle the notion of seeing Easton again.

Until then, I was planning on inviting Katherine along on Benjamin's trip to Bali. I'd whisk her away until I had the courage to return. Until I was strong enough to face Easton, knowing that when I left here today, he'd never forgive me.

"Take care of yourself."

She gave me a sad smile. "Same to you."

I turned away and hurried from her office before she could see my unshed tears. Then I made my way outside to the Cadillac parked in front of the lodge.

I'd tried to find Carol and Liddy earlier, but they'd gone into Missoula for Black Friday shopping, so I'd left them a note. They'd probably hate me for that note, but it was better than hanging around.

The Cadillac was warm when I slid inside, the seats soaking up the early morning sun. I cranked the heat anyway as I started the engine, feeling a cold so deep that I doubted I'd be warm for a hundred miles.

Goddamn it. Why? I wasn't even sure what *why* I was asking. Why was I like this? Why was life so hard? Why didn't he love me? Just . . . why?

My chin quivered and I sucked in a few short breaths, but it was no use. The tears flooded and the world became a glassy blur as I cried into the steering wheel.

What was wrong with me? Why was I leaving?

Because I'm terrified.

The answer came immediately. This time in Montana had woken me up. I was feeling again. I was living. I'd fallen in love.

And I was scared that it would all fall to shit.

If I decided to stay and everything here broke, it would destroy me.

Self-preservation was kicking in, and foolish or not, habits were hard to break. I'd been taking care of myself— depending on myself, protecting myself—for a long, long time.

I wiped my face dry—taking the makeup I'd put on this morning away with the tears—then I took a deep breath, sat up straight and put the Cadillac in reverse.

The road was covered with last night's dusting of snow. There was only one set of tracks to mark the path, probably from Carol and Liddy. Before I could stop myself, I glanced in the rearview mirror, seeing the lodge grow smaller in the distance. Then I rounded a turn and it disappeared behind a towering wall of evergreens.

My hand came to my chest, rubbing my sternum to try and erase the sting.

I pushed the Cadillac faster. Snowy roads or not, it was time to rip off the bandage and get the hell off Greer property.

A billow of snow rose up behind me as I picked up speed and ahead, the highway came into view. The pressure in my chest was nearly crippling, but I breathed through it with both hands locked on the wheel.

Then a black streak caught my eye.

I blinked, once, then twice, and tried to make sense of what I was seeing.

There was a man on a horse, racing along the barbed wire fence that bordered the highway. He was flying.

I gasped, a hand flying to my mouth as my foot lifted off the gas pedal.

Jigsaw was running flat-out, his legs stretching in front of him as he galloped. And on his back, Easton rode with a fluid grace that was so stunningly beautiful, I barely noticed that I'd brought the Cadillac to a full stop.

Easton turned Jigsaw as he neared the road but didn't ease off the pace. He didn't slow until he was close enough for me to see his flushed cheeks, his panted breaths, and that he wasn't wearing a coat.

He leapt off Jigsaw, the animal breathing as hard as his owner, and while the horse stood by waiting, Easton strode to the Cadillac and ripped open the door.

His face was a storm. His eyes blazing.

He was livid. *Fantastic.*

The reason he'd run me down was probably because I'd stolen his shirt.

Easton jerked his thumb over his shoulder. "Out."

Okay, not livid. Murderous.

I eased out of the car, watching as he fisted his hands on his hips and hauled in a few deep breaths.

Easton ripped the cowboy hat off his head and tossed it on the ground. There was sweat at his temples and the temperature was below zero.

"Where's your coat?"

That question earned me an icy glare. "I saw you in the parking lot. Crying."

"Oh." I should have traveled farther to hide my tears. "So?"

He raked a hand through his hair. "I've been waiting over a month for you to figure it out. And you still haven't."

"Figure what out?" That he didn't want me enough to ask me to stay?

He took a step closer and I had the perfect view of his ticking jaw. "Where do you fit, Gemma?"

"Why are you doing this?" Was he trying to hurt me? How could he ask me that question when he knew I didn't have the answer?

"Where do you fit?" he repeated.

Nowhere. I clamped my mouth shut and lifted my chin. Hadn't we done enough of this last night? Did he really need to pick a fight when I was seconds away from leaving him to his life?

Easton stepped forward, closing the distance between us and lifting a hand to my cheek. Then his voice dropped to barely a whisper. "Where do you fit, Gemma?"

The gentleness of his touch melted away my anger. "I don't know."

"Guess."

I shrugged. "On the ranch?"

Easton shook his head and *damn him*, it shattered my heart.

I tried to step away but he had me pinned. "East—"

"With. Me." He dropped his forehead to mine. "You fit right here with me."

A sob escaped, followed by another, and as the tears streamed down my face, he pulled me into his arms. "I don't want to leave."

"Then come home. Please."

"I thought you weren't going to beg me to stay."

"Let me rephrase. Come. Home. That's not me begging. That's me giving orders."

I laughed and cried, burrowing into his shirt as he held me tight.

"I don't want you to go, Gem. Stay."

"Okay," I whispered.

The tension in his frame vanished and he loosened his hold enough to catch my lips.

He licked at the seam and kissed me slow and soft. It was maybe the sweetest gesture he'd shown but my mind was whirling, and it was hard to concentrate on the taste of his tongue and the heat of his breath.

How was this happening? Had he really raced up to me on his horse—his freaking horse—and now I was kissing him? This was one of those moments I'd replay in my head for years to come and still not believe it had been real.

When he pulled away from my lips, I studied his face, trying to make sense of it all. "Why? What made you change your mind and come after me?"

"I was in the stables, pissed at you. I wasn't supposed to be there but my truck got a flat this morning and instead of calling for help, I hiked back."

"Because you were pissed at me," I muttered.

"Yep. Well, I'd just walked in and happened to look over. There you were. Crying and . . ." His eyes melted into dark chocolate pools. "Breaks me to see you cry."

So he'd ridden after me.

He must have come straight from the stables toward the highway, because as the crow flies, it was the fastest way off the ranch. Lucky for me, the road curved and wound its way, otherwise, I would have missed him.

"I don't want to trap you here," he said. "That's why I didn't ask. That's why I said what I said last night. You went through enough. After you told me about your mother, I thought on it and I just . . . I don't ever want you to live somewhere you don't want to be."

That was why he'd gotten strange after my confession? Not because of what I'd told him, but because he'd been worried for me.

He'd been willing to let me go because he'd wanted me to be happy.

"I love you," I blurted.

"I love you." He grinned. "I fucking love you, woman. I'm going to marry you. I'm going to have babies with you. I'm going to fight with you. I'm going to kiss you every morning. And show you every day that this is exactly where you belong."

I wanted it. Every word. Every promise. "Are you asking me to marry you?"

He arched an eyebrow. "Did I ask?"

I laughed and stood on my toes to brush a kiss to his lips. "Let's pretend you did and that I said yes."

Easton's smile stretched across his face. It was the most honest, real smile I'd seen from this man and instantly made me smile back. He only let me appreciate that smile for a second, then his lips were on mine again and there was nothing sweet about our kiss. It was consuming. Branding. Claiming.

I was his. I belonged with him.

The chaos I'd felt for, well . . . forever, seemed to simply uncoil.

Easton kissed me until we were both breathless, then he let me go and jerked his chin to the Cadillac. "Now get back in the car before you freeze. I need to get Jigsaw to the stables, then I'll meet you at the house."

"Okay." I nodded, hesitant to let him go, but I didn't want him outside either.

"Here." He held up a finger as his other hand dove into his jeans pocket, pulling out his keys. On a leather strap were four keys and a black fob. He twisted off the only brass key and pressed it into my hand. "That's yours."

I stared at it in my palm and the lump in my throat came back.

He'd given me the key to his home.

Most people wouldn't be stunned speechless by a key. But I wasn't most people.

Whenever I'd needed a home, I'd gone out and found or built or bought one myself.

And Easton had just given me his.

He kissed my forehead and clicked his tongue to Jigsaw, who hadn't so much as moved from the spot where he'd been left. With a fast swing up, Easton was in the saddle and loping down the road, not wasting any time as he made his way to the stables.

I climbed back in my car, Easton's key clutched in my hand, and drove toward his house.

A smile tugged at my cheeks as I pulled into the space in his driveway, parking in front of the garage. Londyn was going to love this. So was Katherine. So was Benjamin, though I was still going to send him and Taylor to Bali.

I decided to leave my suitcase in the trunk—Easton would haul it in later—and walked up the steps to the porch and to the front entrance, slipping my key inside the lock. I held my breath as I turned the bronze knob, not sure what to expect on the other side of the hickory door. But when I stepped across the threshold, my jaw dropped.

Easton's home was picture perfect. The open floor

plan gave me a view of the wide, expansive kitchen. It flowed seamlessly from the dining area to the living room, filled with leather furniture and walnut pieces. The bay windows in the front of the house were as impressive as those showcasing the view behind the house.

The style was rustic and woodsy, very Easton, yet not overly manly. It was warm and inviting. It was exactly what I would have designed for a home at the base of a mountain.

I took another step inside, closing the door behind me. If Easton had wanted to give me the tour, he'd have to live with the disappointment. The guest bedrooms on the main floor were down a hallway off the living room along with a sparsely decorated office. I peeked into the pantry along with both the mud and laundry rooms.

When I walked down the hallway leading to the back of the house, Easton's scent greeted me before I stepped into the enormous, master suite.

His bed was unmade. The charcoal sheets were rumpled and the suede quilt strewn on the floor. Every night he'd spent at the cabin, he'd slept like a rock, barely moving. Which meant last night, he'd probably tossed and turned.

I walked deeper into the bedroom, not bothering with the light. He'd vaulted the ceiling in the bedroom and the back wall was made almost entirely of glass. Sunbeams streamed inside, lighting the room and warming my face.

Every step felt heavy. Deep. Like with each one, my

feet sank through the hardwood floor, past the concrete foundation and into the earth.

Like a tree's roots taking hold.

A wave of emotion welled in my chest and I was crying again. Damn it, I'd cried more in the past twenty-four hours than I had in the last eleven years.

Maybe that was expected when someone like me finally found it.

Home.

I hadn't cried for long when two arms banded around me and Easton pulled me into his chest. "You okay?"

I nodded, leaning into his embrace. "They're happy tears."

"Good. Welcome home, darlin'."

EPILOGUE

GEMMA

Six months later . . .

"I don't like the doctor."

Easton chuckled. "At last week's appointment, you loved her. You invited her to the wedding."

"She can forget that invitation now."

He reached across the cab of the truck and took my hand, holding it as we bumped down the road. "We'll get the car to California. It's just not going to be for a while."

"A long while." My shoulders fell. "I need to call Londyn."

"She's not going to care."

"She might."

He lifted my hand to his lips and kissed my knuckles. "She won't."

My fiancé was right. Londyn wouldn't care about the car. Hell, she'd had it in West Virginia for a year before I'd taken it on my adventure. Mostly, I was pouting because the doctor's news was not what I'd hoped to hear.

As of today, I was on activity rest. I'd be trapped inside the house for months while I finished growing this baby. And the trip that we'd planned to take to California in three weeks was on hiatus. Neither Easton nor I would risk being on the road with the warning light on this pregnancy.

"I hate this," I muttered. "I'm scared."

He looked across the cab. "It's going to be okay."

"What if we can't get my blood pressure down?"

"We will."

I found it cruelly ironic. If the doctor didn't want me stressed during the remainder of my pregnancy, she shouldn't have told me all the bad stuff that could happen.

She was definitely not invited to our wedding.

The day Easton had stopped me from leaving and given me his caveman proposal, we'd spent alone at the house. He'd brought in my things and had helped me unpack, moving me into his house—our house. And that night, he'd insisted we go to family dinner.

We'd walked in the door at Carol and Jake's, and before anyone could react to the fact that I wasn't on my way to California or scold me for leaving a note, he'd announced we were engaged.

Two weeks later, he'd come home with a diamond ring.

Two weeks after that, I'd come home with pregnancy

tests.

So far, this pregnancy had been a cakewalk. I hadn't had any morning sickness and my energy levels had been great. But two weeks ago, I'd gone in for a routine checkup and the doctor had worried that my blood pressure was higher than normal. This week was more of the same. If next week's checkup was a continuation, I'd have to take medication, something I'd avoided completely since my pregnancy test had shown positive.

I was eating healthy. I was getting exercise. But the anxiety of growing a human and becoming a mother was getting to me.

I hadn't exactly had a good role model during my formative years.

"I just want the baby to be okay." I stroked my belly, taking deep breaths.

"He will be." Easton clutched my hand. "You both will be."

It would be easier to believe him if his nerves weren't coming through his voice and there wasn't a worry line between his eyebrows.

Easton was over the moon that we were having a boy. Last month, he'd gone into Missoula with the trailer to pick up some specialty mineral supplements for the livestock, and while he'd been at the farm and ranch supply store, he'd found a pair of baby cowboy boots. And a baby cowboy hat. And a baby pair of felt chaps.

The getup was currently in the nursery closet,

awaiting the day when he'd be old enough to wear them and I'd take a million photos.

Easton had also told Cash that the best colt born this year was ours.

Maybe I hadn't had good parents, but I was lucky that the man at my side would more than compensate for my shortcomings. And we could lean into our family.

The Greers were as excited about this baby as we were.

We pulled up to Carol and Jake's place and Easton shut off the truck. We were late for family dinner because my appointment had gone long, but it was a gorgeous evening.

The May flowers were in full bloom, the front of Carol's flower beds brimming with canary-yellow daffodils and fuchsia tulips. The ranch was as green as I'd ever seen it, the meadows lush and the trees overflowing with blossoms.

Calves danced around their mother's legs. Fawns bounded through the grass. JR and Liddy had a batch of baby chicks and there was a litter of new barn cats.

And soon, I prayed, we'd have a healthy and happy baby boy.

"Don't get out," Easton ordered. "I'll come around and help."

Normally, that would earn him an eye-roll. But tonight, I'd listen because he was worried and I knew he felt helpless.

As he opened my door, I swung my legs to the side and took his face in my hands. "I love you."

He leaned in, sliding his arms around me and tucking his head against my neck. "I love you too."

We held on to each other until the front door opened and Cash called, "Granddad wants to know if you both want cheese on your burgers."

"I'm pregnant. What kind of stupid-ass question is that?"

Easton laughed and leaned away to holler at Cash. "Yes, cheese."

"Double on mine!"

He grinned and helped me to the ground, then pinned me to his side as we walked to the house. The minute we crossed the threshold, we were bombarded with questions about my appointment. Carol ushered me to a chair at the dining room table, Liddy brought me a glass of iced water and Katherine sat down beside me.

Easton dropped a kiss to my cheek, then disappeared outside to find the guys who were hovering beside the grill, while I gave a recap of my appointment.

"So I guess this means your trip is canceled," Katherine said.

"Yes." I sighed. "I'll call Londyn later and tell her."

"She won't care."

"I know. It's just disappointing." I'd been looking forward to the trip, not only to find Karson, but because Easton would be going with me.

When—if—I decided to see my mother, I wouldn't have had to face her alone.

I shrugged. "Eventually, we'll go."

It would be after the baby was born, and after the wedding we'd planned for next June. Maybe this road trip to California could be part of our honeymoon.

Carol, Liddy and Katherine had thrown themselves into the wedding planning. The four of us met each Sunday to go through bridal magazines and talk about ideas. They were anxious to make me an official Greer, though I didn't need the last name to feel a part of this family. Every day that went by, those roots grew deeper.

I'd been dealt a miserable set of cards for the first part of my life, but now I was getting straight aces.

"Can I help with dinner?" I asked, practically begging not to have to sit here while people waited on me.

Carol scoffed. Liddy gave me a sweet smile while shaking her head. Katherine hid her laugh in a glass of wine.

"Activity restrictions," I muttered. "This sucks."

And if I knew Easton, he was outside right now talking to his grandfather, father and brother about how to cut my hours at the training facility.

The expansion was in full swing on the new property, with Cash taking the lead. We'd planned to take the trip to California in a few weeks because it would be before the construction crew broke ground on the stables at the new training facility.

Once construction started, I didn't want to miss a minute, especially after contributing a million dollars to the project. It was the first of three major investments I'd made in the past six months, though with the other two I truly was silent.

One was a women's shelter in California for women who'd escaped their nightmares. Dr. Brewer had recommended the organization to me and they'd been thrilled to welcome me aboard. The other was a national children's organization that focused on serving runaway kids. I'd been happy to give them large sums of money and let them run with the dollars.

Benjamin had been more than happy to take them under his wing so I could concentrate on activities in Montana.

The expansion would be time consuming for us all to get it off the ground, though particularly so for Cash and me. Easton thought the expansion was part of my elevated stress levels. He wasn't entirely wrong.

If they voted to have me station the lodge's front desk again, I was moving back to the cabin.

Not long after Christmas, the time spent planning the training facility had ramped up. On top of the already busy resort and ranch activities, Easton and Cash had struggled to keep up with the emails and phone calls and general office work.

Enter me.

I loved barking orders and making decisions and as it

turned out, my entrepreneurial expertise came in handy, so I'd been promoted from silent investor to joint director of operations. Cash and I were working together to get the breeding and training facility open. We were having a blast, though the hours had been demanding.

Maybe too demanding.

But it was hard to slow down when everyone was so excited. When *I* was excited. This was more than just my new job. This was more than turning a profit. This was about building a legacy for my son.

"Promise you won't make me sit at the front—" Before I could get Katherine on my side in this inevitable war about what was best for Gemma, the doorbell rang.

"Who could that be?" Carol stood from the table, but before she could take a step, Cash flew inside.

"I got it. I got it. I got it." He waved us all back into our seats and rushed to the door. He swung it open and a female voice floated through the air.

My stomach dropped and I turned to Katherine, seeing all the blood drain from her face as Cash escorted a pretty blonde into the house.

Holding her hand.

No. Cash, you idiot.

Katherine's eyes were glued to their linked hands. She studied them for a long moment as Carol and Liddy greeted the guest, surprised as we were by the addition.

"You guys remember Dany?" Cash asked, getting nods.

"Hey, Kat." Dany waved.

"Hey." Katherine forced a smile but it didn't reach her eyes.

I stood, using my growing belly to block out Katherine and give her a chance to recover. "Hey, Dany. I'm Gemma. Nice to meet you."

"Nice to meet you too."

I let go of her hand just as Easton came inside carrying a platter of burgers.

He saved me from making small talk and with everyone clustered around the table, fixing their burgers and diving into the meal, it allowed Katherine time to pretend this wasn't killing her.

I loved Cash. We'd gotten to know each other these past six months and he was genuinely a good man, like his brother. But for fuck's sake, he was stupid when it came to women.

What on earth had possessed him to bring a woman tonight? Who was this Dany? And when had they started dating? The two of them sat side by side at the dinner table, whispering and canoodling and annoying the hell out of the rest of us.

I nudged Easton's elbow with my own, then shot him a silent question. Had he known about this?

He shook his head, as shocked as the rest of us.

The minute her burger was done, Katherine took her plate to the kitchen without a word. I stood to follow.

"Leave your plate," Carol said.

"It's an empty plate." I ignored her and found Katherine in the kitchen, refilling her glass of wine. "Hey."

"Hey."

"I take it this was a surprise."

She nodded and gulped her wine.

"Sorry."

"It's fine."

"Liar."

Katherine hung her head. "I'm so stupid. I mean, I knew this would happen eventually. I just hoped . . ."

That Cash would love her, like she loved him.

"I can't keep doing this," she whispered. "Waiting. I need—I don't know what I need."

"A vacation." An idea sparked.

It happened to me every so often—where something hit me with such force that I knew instantly it would be brilliant. Like the time I'd sunk an entire year's profit at Gemma Lane into development of an organic, eco-friendly skin care line. It had paid off tenfold within thirteen months.

"I don't have time for a vacation," she said.

"You need to make time. Get away from here. Get away from him. Carol and Liddy and JR will cover for you. Let your heart heal a little bit."

Her eyes tracked to the dining room where Dany had said something to make Cash burst out laughing. "Where would I go?"

"Drive the Cadillac to California."

"No," she said instantly. "I'm never going back there."

I didn't blame her for that. "Then how about, um . . ." I snapped my fingers. "Oregon."

"What's in Oregon?" she asked.

"Not what, but *who*." I smiled. "Aria."

"Huh?"

"Take the car to Aria. It's fitting, don't you think? I took the Cadillac from Londyn. You can take it from me. And if you don't want to go to California, I bet Aria would. Give her the car."

"How do you know? Have you talked to her?"

"Well, no. But worst case, she doesn't want to, and you return home with a car. Then once the baby is old enough, Easton and I will drive it and find Karson."

"How do you know Aria's still in Oregon?"

"Well, I don't. But it wouldn't be hard to find out." One call to my private investigator and we'd know before breakfast.

"What about Londyn?"

"You said it earlier. She's not going to care."

Katherine sipped her wine, thinking it over. Then her eyes went to the dining room once more just in time to see Cash drop a kiss to Dany's forehead. "Okay. I'll go. Give me a day to get things in order."

Oh my God, it worked. I thought it would take more convincing. "Great! We'll have the car ready to go."

She nodded and set her wine aside, then she walked out of the kitchen, not headed toward the group, but straight for the door. She paused with her hand on the knob and looked back. "Thanks."

"You're welcome."

I stayed put, watching as she slipped out.

"Damn." Easton sighed, appearing at my side. "She's upset."

"Yeah."

He put his arm around my shoulders, pulling me close. "How are you?"

"Full. Tired." I leaned into him. "Ready to go home."

"Okay." He kept hold of me as he called into the dining room, "We're taking off. Kat's headed home too."

After a round of goodbyes and a plastic container of chocolate chip cookies, we drove home with the windows down, savoring the fragrant spring air.

"Katherine's going to drive the Cadillac to Oregon," I told him.

"Alone? When?"

"Well . . ." I took a deep breath and told him my plan.

My whole plan.

What I'd told Katherine had only been a part of my grand scheme.

"You sure this is a good idea?" he asked as we walked into our house and he tossed his keys on the kitchen island.

"Positive. This will work."

"For Katherine's sake, and Cash's, I hope you're right."

"Me too." I rubbed my belly, feeling the baby kick. "Ooh. Come here."

Easton came closer and I took his hand, positioning his palm on my side. We stilled, waiting, then another kick jabbed in just the right spot.

"Did you feel that?"

His eyes softened, his palm never moving as his free arm wrapped around me and he dropped his cheek to my head. "It's going to be okay."

"Yeah. It's going to be okay." I sank into his side.

I'd work the boring front desk and let Cash handle the expansion. I'd stop spending late nights in our home office. I'd take up reading or crochet or prenatal yoga. And if needed, I'd go on the medication.

Because this baby was worth every sacrifice in the world.

"It's going to be more than okay."

———

TWO AND A HALF MONTHS LATER, our son was born. Jake Easton Greer joined the world in perfect health with a mat of my brown hair and his father's dark eyes.

And that real life I'd been searching for . . .

It had been in Montana the whole time.

Waiting for me to come home.

———

The Runaway series continues with Quarter Miles.

QUARTER MILES

Katherine Gates has been in love with Cash Greer since the moment he saved her life from a runaway goat. According to Cash, she's the little sister he never had, the greatest roommate in the world and his favorite coworker. They're friends—best friends.

In the dark days of her youth, it was her friendships that kept her alive and made life in a junkyard worth living. So she's learned to shove her feelings for Cash down deep, even if that means ignoring eyes that shine brighter than the Montana summer sun and the smile that illuminates the snowiest winter day.

Except with every passing year, the denial takes its toll on her wounded heart until one day Katherine decides to take an impulsive road trip to the Oregon coast. Alone. That is, until Cash cons his way into the passenger seat.

The farther they travel, the harder it is to pretend. And when she confesses her feelings, she learns that Cash has some secrets of his own. Secrets that will either bond them together.

Or rip them apart.

ACKNOWLEDGMENTS

Thank you for reading *Wild Highway*! The Runaway series is such a blast for me to write and I'm so very grateful you picked up a copy.

Special thanks to my editing and proofreading team: Marion Archer, Julie Deaton, Karen Lawson and Judy Zweifel. Thank you to Sarah Hansen for the cover—both of them. Thanks to my agent, Kimberly Brower. To the Goldbrickers, thanks for keeping me on track and motivating me each day. And thank you to my publicist, Danielle Sanchez, for everything you do.

Perry Street, you are the best reader group in the world. Your love and support mean everything to me. Thank you to the amazing bloggers who read and promote my books.

With every book release, I send a million virtual hugs into the universe for all you do. I hope you feel them.

And lastly, to my friends and family. I don't know how I got so lucky to have you all in my corner. Thanks for believing in me every single day.

ABOUT THE AUTHOR

Devney is a *USA Today* bestselling author who lives in Washington with her husband and two sons. Born and raised in Montana, she loves writing books set in her treasured home state. After working in the technology industry for nearly a decade, she abandoned conference calls and project schedules to enjoy a slower pace at home with her family. Writing one book, let alone many, was not something she ever expected to do. But now that she's discovered her true passion for writing romance, she has no plans to ever stop.

Don't miss out on Devney's latest book news.
Subscribe to her newsletter!
www.devneyperry.com